#2

JUNIOR HIGH

CLASS CRUSH

JUNIOR HIGH

#2

JUNIOR HIGH

CLASS CRUSH

Kate Kenyon

SCHOLASTIC INC.
New York Toronto London Auckland Sydney

ISBN 0-590-41649-9

Copyright © 1987 by Jacqueline Shannon. All rights
reserved. Published by Scholastic Inc. JUNIOR HIGH
is a trademark of Scholastic Inc.

12 11 10 9 8 7 6 5   2/9

Printed in the U.S.A.

01

First Scholastic printing, January 1987

Chapter 1

"I am madly, impossibly, completely, totally, one-hundred percent, forever, head over heels in love," said Nora Ryan.

Jennifer Mann looked across the table at her best friend and laughed. "I take it you sort of like the guy." Then her eyes went as dreamy as Nora's. "He *is* gorgeous, isn't he?"

"And there he is!" squealed Tracy Douglas.

Susan Hillard slapped Tracy's hand. "Shh! He'll hear you, dummy. Don't be so obvious!"

But like the others, Susan craned her neck to watch Mr. Rochester cross the Cedar Groves Junior High cafeteria with long strides.

Jennifer took her eyes off the new English teacher long enough to really look at the cafeteria, something she hadn't done since her first day at Cedar Groves Junior

High. Suddenly she was embarrassed that Mr. Rochester was seeing dull pea-soup-green walls, a water-stained ceiling, and a dingy linoleum floor. "He seems so out of place here," Jennifer murmured aloud.

Nora stopped watching Mr. Rochester long enough for an appreciative glance at Jennifer. As usual, it was as if they had read each other's minds! But what can you expect when you've been best friends since kindergarten? Nora thought.

Mr. Rochester stopped at the door to the teacher's dining room and threw one last look over his shoulder with his piercing black eyes. Then he brushed a lock of black hair off his forehead and disappeared through the door.

Tracy sighed as she dug into her bowl of chili. "Have you ever seen anybody look so good in a fishnet sweater?"

"It's called a *fisherman knit* sweater," Susan snorted.

Tracy didn't hear her over the noise of banging trays and silverware that surrounded their favorite center table. "How lucky can the eighth grade get?" she asked.

"Wrong again," Susan snapped. "It's not called luck, it's called 'maternity leave.' Seems to me we would have been luckier if Mrs. Rickerts hadn't waited till the last minute to leave. Then we would have known Mr. Rochester for two months already instead of just two hours."

"Well," Nora said, "clinically speaking, she should be out at least — "

"Can it, Doctor Ryan!" The others laughingly cut her off. Nora did, beaming. "Doctor Ryan" sounded so good! And someday, after medical school, the title would *really* be hers!

"Mrs. Rickerts told me she'd be out for the rest of this semester and all of next," Jennifer said. "I'm glad the poor thing is taking time off. Caring for a new baby is probably a lot of work."

"I bet he likes blondes," Tracy said, patting her own blonde hair.

For a few seconds, Nora thought Tracy was referring to Mrs. Rickerts' baby. When she realized that Tracy meant Mr. Rochester, she burst out laughing. How could she forget that Tracy had a one-track mind and that the only thing running around that track were males?

Tracy misunderstood Nora's laughter and looked hurt. "What's so funny about that? They say opposites attract, you know."

"Then you're a shoo-in in at least one category," Susan jeered. "I mean, Mr. Rochester is obviously very intelligent."

Jennifer swallowed a mouthful of Jell-O. "I hope it's the other way around," she said quickly to distract Tracy before Susan's words sunk in. "I mean, I hope it's people who *aren't* opposites that attract."

Nora looked at her friend and saw what she meant. Like the teacher, Jennifer was tall and slender with fair skin and black hair.

"At least your eyes are hazel and not black," Nora said, her own brown eyes dancing.

"And at least you're *short*," Jennifer shot back.

The two stared at each other, surprised to find themselves acting and sounding like rivals! Then they laughed. Laughing always makes it okay between us, Jennifer thought. A second later, however, Nora was kicking her under the table. "*Stop laughing!*" Nora hissed. Jennifer did, and as she looked up, she understood the warning. Mia Stevens and Andy Warwick were drifting over to their table.

Mia, the female half of Cedar Groves Junior High's punk couple, was wearing a new yellow rain slicker — the exact same kind Jen's dad had bought her and that she hated, because it made her look about eight years old. Mia, however, had turned hers into a plastic minidress by fastening a huge neon-green belt around her waist and hacking off the sleeves. It looked so different from the innocent-looking original that Jennifer and Nora could hardly keep from laughing in front of Mia.

"Guess what Mr. Rochester said to me after class today!" Mia was excitedly pulling at her spiky hair, some of which was streaked the same bright yellow as the ex-raincoat. "He said I look like Exene Cervenka, the lead singer of X! Can you believe that? A teacher who knows about X!"

Andy sighed and shook his own spiky head, which was about the same neon-green as Mia's belt. "Can't you talk about anything besides this Rochester cat, Mia? I've heard that Exene story five times!"

Mia sat down at the table. "I say he's not married," she said, ignoring Andy. He shrugged and wandered off.

"What makes you think that?" Jennifer asked.

Mia held up her hand and wiggled her fingers; her nails were painted a warm forest green. "No wedding ring."

"Wait!" Nora said, waving her hands. "That doesn't mean anything. My dad has a wedding ring but doesn't wear it. He says he's afraid he'll catch it on something and lose the finger."

Jennifer sighed. "It isn't fair. Married people should have to wear their wedding rings."

"What are you guys talking about?"

Everyone looked up at the sound of the sweet, slightly accented voice of Denise

Hendrix. As Nora explained about the problem of telling whether someone was married or not, Jennifer studied Denise. For the millionth time, she decided Denise was the most beautiful girl she had ever seen. Her perfect, heart-shaped face was framed by golden hair that today cascaded onto a big, bulky sweater the exact color of her cornflower-blue eyes. She doesn't look like she belongs in this cafeteria, either, Jennifer thought. She looks like she belongs in a . . . well, in a Swiss boarding school! Which is exactly where Denise had been until her family had moved to Cedar Groves the past summer.

"When I went to a ball in London last spring, every unmarried man was announced as 'Master,' " Denise was saying. "I guess that's pretty standard in the British upper class."

"What do you mean by 'announced'?" Nora asked.

"When people came through the door, the butler would call out 'Master John Davis,' 'Mr. and Mrs. Lamont Thurston,' 'Master Ronald Conrad,' and so on," Denise explained, a little impatiently.

"Well, pardon us for not doing much jet-setting lately," Susan snapped. "School gets in the way."

Jennifer saw Denise's expression turn wistful. The wealthy Hendrix family owned

Denise Cosmetics, one of the biggest companies in the world. They had lived and traveled all over Europe . . . until the day Mr. and Mrs. Hendrix decided that Denise and her sixteen-year-old brother Tony should grow up as Americans.

"You should have seen all the girls turn and stare when the butler announced 'Master Tony Hendrix,'" Denise said. "He looks gorgeous in a tuxedo."

She paused and was surprised when nobody — not even Tracy — pressed her for more details about her brother Tony as they usually did. Nobody even made a general remark about what a hunk he was.

"Let's just hope it's *Master* Rochester," Mia said, and Jen, Nora, Tracy, and Susan nodded.

Suddenly, Denise figured out the reason for the discussion. "Oh, no," she groaned, slapping her forehead. "Not a teacher crush! Teacher crushes are *so* seventh grade!"

Nora and Jennifer exchanged looks and shrugs that said What did you expect? The Hendrix family's many moves had put Denise a year behind in school, so she was fourteen instead of thirteen like the other eighth-graders. It was only a year's difference, but it sometimes felt like five to Nora and Jennifer. Denise was so much more sophisticated about things — like guys.

She'd actually already had several dates, both in Europe and in Cedar Groves.

"We *don't* have a crush on Mr. Rochester," Susan said coldly. "We just happen to be talking about him, that's all."

But Denise wasn't fooled. "Just don't go building him up into something he's not, you guys. Because you'll end up terribly disappointed, I promise."

She launched into a tale about a crush she and several other girls had had on a young math teacher at Chateau Remy, the boarding school she had attended in Switzerland.

"He had this mysterious air about him and really troubled eyes," Denise said dramatically. "We thought he must be trying to get over a tragic love affair, that maybe his fiancée had died in a plane crash or something."

She went on to describe in detail the elaborate surprise party they'd thrown for the teacher, hoping to cheer him up.

"It turned out he just had stomach problems — that was the reason for the troubled eyes and airs," Denise said with a sigh. "At the party, he was really crabby and refused to eat anything but a roll of antacids that fell out of his pocket. And eight girls fell out of love."

"Sometimes antacids can actually aggravate an ulcerous condition," Nora said.

Everyone knew what was coming. "Not during lunch, Nora!" pleaded Susan.

"I think this is a good time to leave for the girls' room," Denise said.

Nora just smiled. "You see, the stomach lining is — "

" — is not going to be discussed, thanks to me!" said Lucy Armanson, laughing, as she joined the group at the table. "I'm sure you'd rather hear the juicy information I picked up about your Mr. Rochester in the office a few minutes ago."

"So tell us!" the others pleaded.

Lucy grinned and shook her shiny black Afro. "Only on one condition. Nora has to promise not to give me a nutritional lecture about these!" She opened her purse and took out a package of Twinkies.

Even Nora laughed. "It's a deal," she said. "But just this once." Lucy, as usual, looked to Nora like she'd stepped out of the fashion pages of *Seventeen*, her slender frame and high cheekbones emphasized by a burgundy sweater dress with a cowl neck.

Lucy made a face at Nora and then turned serious. "Well, the bad news is — " She paused dramatically, and the others stopped breathing. " — he's married."

The girls let their breaths out in a groan. "Oh, nooo!"

"Sorry, but he is," Lucy said, tearing open the Twinkies package. "I heard him say 'Edna and I are settling in just fine' to Mrs. Peters."

"*Edna?*" Mia said. "Yuck!"

"How could such a gorgeous man marry someone with such an ugly first name?" Tracy wailed.

"Speaking of first names, guess what Mr. Rochester's is?" Lucy said. She couldn't wait. "Cliff!"

"Oh!" Tracy squealed. "How romantic!"

"Now *that* fits," Nora said. "Cliff Rochester."

Most of the other girls tried the name out loud, too, so they barely noticed the sudden arrival of a freckled face topped by red hair. Jason Anthony dipped his finger into Jennifer's Jell-O and licked it before going on to sample Tracy's chili the same way. To his surprise, nobody complained.

What's with them? Jason wondered. Where were the usual shouts of grossed-out protest? Where were the usual mutterings of "terminal creep," or "pencil-necked geek," or even a mild "borderline defective"? He took a quick bite off of the Twinkie Lucy was gesturing with and was stunned when she simply handed it to him and went on talking about some cliff. Jason glanced at the other girls around the table and spotted a head of curly brown hair. Aha — Nora! He could always get a rise out of Nora. He went around the table and put a large thumbprint on her half-eaten bran muffin.

Much to Jason's relief, Nora absent-mindedly picked up a book and swatted at him. Jason grabbed it away from her and looked at the title: *Wuthering Heights*.

"Oh, am I wuthering you?" he asked, laughing heartily at his wit. No one even groaned!

Instead, Nora grabbed the book back and pointed at the cover excitely. "Look how much Cliff looks like Heathcliff!"

Jennifer peered at it. "Oh, you're *right*! What a coincidence that he assigned it to us."

Susan lifted her nose into the air haughtily and cleared her throat. "A-hem! *I* saw the physical resemblance hours ago," she said. "But I'm sure I'm the *only* one of us who also realizes that Cliff Rochester's name is a combination of two of the Bronte sisters' main characters: Heathcliff from Emily Bronte's *Wuthering Heights* and Edward Rochester from Charlotte Bronte's *Jane Eyre*."

Everyone stared silently at Susan.

"But how could I have expected you to know that?" Susan continued. "After all, I'm sure I'm the only person here who's ever read either book — and I've read them at least twenty times apiece. They're my favorite books in the whole world . . . just like they're Cliff's favorites! You *did* hear him say that this morning, didn't you?"

Nora, Jennifer, and Mia nodded.

"So you see, I'm the only one of us who really has anything in common with him," Susan finished smugly.

Nora shook a finger at her. "You don't know if — "

"*I'm* going to call him Heathcliff," Susan announced, cutting her off.

"But Cliff said Heathcliff is a *mean* character," Jennifer protested.

Susan flashed her a cold little smile. "I like mean characters."

Tracy was still stuck on Susan's statement about the Bronte sisters. "Jane Air . . . Jane Air . . . didn't I read something about her in *People* magazine last week?" she asked.

Susan faked a gasp. "You mean you've actually learned to read?" She picked up her tray and flounced away from the table.

Jennifer kindly explained to Tracy that *Jane Eyre* was a book.

"Oh," Tracy said. "Why couldn't *Susan* have told me that instead of making fun of me? She *always* has to make fun of me!"

Lucy patted her shoulder. "It's no wonder Susan likes mean characters — she *is* one. That girl never has anything nice to say about anyone."

Chapter 2

Fifty-three seconds after the final bell rang that same afternoon, Nora had already shrugged into her coat, slammed her locker shut, and grabbed Jennifer's arm. "Come *on*, or we'll miss him!" she panted, out of breath from running out of her last class.

Jennifer shook herself free and gently closed her own locker. "Nora, wait. . . ." Thoughtfully, she ran a finger along one edge of the "Save the Whales" bumpersticker she'd plastered on the front of her locker. "I have this weird feeling I'm forgetting to do something . . . or bring something home . . . or something."

"Think about it on our way to the parking lot," Nora said. "Do you want to miss seeing what kind of car Cliff drives?"

Jennifer shook her head as if to clear it. "I sure don't. Okay . . . let's go!" This time she grabbed Nora's arm and the two girls ran, dodging bodies, down the main corridor, which was becoming more of a mob scene by the second. As they careened around a corner, Jennifer crashed into Mitch Pauley.

Laughing, Mitch reached out and grabbed her to keep her from falling. Then he picked up the shoulder bag Jennifer had dropped in the collision. "Now that's what I like — a girl who can tackle!" he said, handing it to her. Jennifer barely glanced at the tall, dark-eyed boy who had been voted the school's best all-around athlete. Mitch watched in surprise as she simply ran off to catch up with Nora, who hadn't said so much as "hi" to him, either!

Still puzzled, he waved absently as Tommy Ryder approached from the same direction Jennifer and Nora had run.

"Would somebody tell me what's going on?" Tommy asked, a frown creasing his handsome face. "I just passed a bunch of the girls . . . or I guess I should say they passed me — "

" — And they acted like they were possessed or something?" Mitch finished for him.

Tommy ran a hand through his sandy brown hair. "Yeah! Even Tracy barely batted her eyelashes at me."

"You must be losing your touch, Ryder," Mitch teased, as Jason Anthony whizzed up on his skateboard and circled around them. "I thought you said Tracy was crazy about you."

Tommy finally flashed his famous wide smile, the one he was sure knocked 'em dead. "She is. They *all* are. Must be some kind of virus going around."

Jason jumped off his skateboard so that it flew up and landed in his hands (but only after hitting him on the chin). "It has something to do with that book Rochester assigned."

"*Wuthering Heights*?" Tommy and Mitch asked him in unison.

"Yeah," Jason said. "They were slobbering all over it in the cafeteria. I mean, they were slobbering all over the guy on the cover. Heathcliff."

Mitch narrowed his eyes, puzzled. "They're in love with a book character?"

Jason shrugged. "Guess so. They've even shortened his name to 'Cliff.' " He raised his voice to a falsetto: "Oh, it sounds soooooooo romantic!" he squealed, in a very good imitation of Tracy.

Tommy laughed. "Well, that guy's no competition — after all, he's almost a hundred and fifty years old . . . or something like that!"

"I've heard of girls falling for older men, but this is ridiculous!" Jason added.

"Who are you talking about?" Andy Warwick asked, joining the boys.

Tommy filled him in on the girls' reaction to the book.

"Oh, so *that's* what it was," Andy said, relieved. "The *book*! That's what they were all talking about at lunch." He ran his finger around the inside of the new dog collar he was wearing. "Nora didn't even ask whether this was a flea collar. I actually kinda missed her lecture about how flea repellent has been found to cause allergies in humans. And Mia . . . Mia was acting all weirded out, too. For a while there, I thought she was getting a crush on the teacher, Rochester — "

Mitch and Tommy burst out laughing. "That pale, skinny, old guy?" Tommy interrupted.

"Yeah, but now I see she just likes him because he assigned the stupid book," Andy continued. "Speaking of Mia, have you guys seen her?"

"She was running thataway about five minutes ago," Tommy said, pointing.

"She left without me!" Andy said angrily.

Mitch glanced at his watch. He was expected in the gym for basketball practice in three minutes. "How long do you suppose this weird book crush is gonna last?" he asked.

Tommy grinned. "Twenty-four hours, tops. They'll forget this Heathcliff as soon as they see how often he strolls out of *Wuthering Heights* to buy them ice-cream at Temptations."

"Or to shoot the free throw that wins the game," Mitch said.

Andy nodded, laughing. "The cat's nothing but a cardboard cover who really can't compare to — "

He stopped and watched Jason, belly down on his skateboard, push off down the corridor, using his hands like oars and humming the theme from *Jaws*.

"— well, to *some* of us guys, anyway," Tommy finished for him, shaking his head.

Jennifer and Nora burst through the door and into the teachers' parking lot only to find that Mia, Susan, and Tracy were already there, huddling against the building in the cold late-autumn air.

"Oh no, not more!" Susan groaned.

Nora nudged Jennifer. "I thought we weren't going to tell anyone else about this."

Jennifer sighed. "If you didn't, I don't know who did."

"Great minds think alike, as the saying goes," Nora said. She turned to the others. "Has Cliff come out yet?"

"No, but I saw him locking the — " Mia broke off as the door opened. But it was only Mr. Mario, Nora and Jen's homeroom teacher. He gave the group an odd look before getting into a station wagon and driving away.

"We look so *obvious*," Jennifer wailed.

"Well, *I* don't," Susan snapped. "If Heathcliff asks me what I'm doing here, I'm telling him that this is where my mom picks me up every day. I'm going to say she thinks there's too much traffic in front of the school."

Mia nodded. "I'm going to say that, too."

"Me, too," Tracy said.

"Don't be ridiculous," Susan said angrily. "All of us can't say the same thing! That would really look phony. You guys come up with your own excuses!"

Nora clapped her hands. "I've got it! We'll say your mom is picking *all* of us up, Susan."

Susan thought it over. "Well, okay."

"Gee, I hope your mother has a van, Susan, or we won't all fit," Tracy said.

Susan slapped her forehead with her palm in exasperation.

"Susan's mom isn't really coming, Tracy," Jen said gently.

Suddenly, the door opened and *he* stepped out, shading his eyes from the afternoon glare. Passing the girls, he flashed them a dazzling white smile and headed for a shiny blue Mustang convertible with its top up.

"Wonder what's taking your mom so long, Susan," Nora croaked loudly.

The teacher got into his car. When he started it, the girls could faintly hear Simple Minds' "All the Things She Said."

"That smile!" Mia whispered weakly. "I have Jell-O legs. I need a drink of water. I'm going back in."

"Me, too," Tracy said.

"Nobody move!" Susan hissed. "Wait till he's gone. We're supposed to be waiting for my mother, you idiots." Then her voice softened. "I just *knew* Heathcliff would have a convertible. I bet he leaves the top down if it's even halfway warm. He probably loves the feel of the wind rushing through his hair . . . just like the other Heathcliff did when he rode across the moors on his horse." She hugged herself.

"What are moors?" Mia asked as Cliff backed out of his parking space.

"Rolling land covered with heather," Susan said dreamily, watching Cliff make a left turn out of the lot.

Nora burst out laughing. "Cedar Groves doesn't have any moors." Ignoring Susan's glare, she linked arms with Jennifer and the two went back inside the building.

"Oh, there you are, Jen!" Lucy called as they came out of the school's heavy double front doors a few minutes later. "I was

19

hoping you hadn't left yet. Here's your *Seventeen* back. I forgot to return it at lunch."

Jen took it from her absently. "Guess what, Lucy? Cliff's from Massachusetts, according to his license plates."

"I thought I told you that," Lucy said. "I heard him tell Mrs. Peters he's from somewhere called Marblehead. Isn't that a funny name for a — "

"*Marblehead?*" Jennifer squeaked. Turning to Nora, she crushed her books to her chest and began jumping up and down. "Nora, *Jeff* is from Marblehead, remember? Maybe he knows Cliff!"

Lucy looked at them blankly. "Jeff? Who's Jeff?"

"The Manns' housekeeper," Nora replied. "Jen, wait! Jeff said there were twenty-five thousand people in that town. You can't expect Jeff to know every one of them. Do *you* know twenty-five thousand people? I'd say it's a one in twenty-five thousand shot."

"I don't care," Jen said. "I'm going right home and asking him. Want to come?"

"No, thanks," Lucy said, shaking her head. "I'm swamped with homework. And I think I can live without knowing."

"I'll come," Nora said.

But the two had barely made it to the sidewalk when Jennifer suddenly came to a dead stop. "Oh, Nora, I can't," she said. "I just remembered what I've been trying to remember all afternoon. There's a meeting this afternoon at the orphanage to plan the next puppet show!"

Nobody cares as much as Jen does, Nora found herself thinking admiringly, as always. If she wasn't putting on a puppet show at the orphanage, she was helping to save the whales, or collecting money and clothing for children on an Arizona Indian reservation. And, oh yes, once a month, Jen baked cookies for the Cedar Groves Nursing Home. The elderly residents loved her as much as the kids at the orphanage did. Jennifer also spent Saturday afternoons answering the phone, cleaning cages, and doing other volunteer work at the animal shelter.

But right now, Nora couldn't hold back a sigh of disappointment. "Are you sure it's today?"

Jennifer nodded. "Positive. The twenty-eighth at four o'clock."

Nora whooped with delight. "But today's the twenty-*seventh*," she shouted happily.

They took off down the street, laughing.

Jeff Crawford was stirring a pot of goulash on the stove when Nora and Jennifer burst into the Manns' sparkling blue-and-white kitchen.

"Jeff!" Jennifer called breathlessly. "Do you know a man named Cliff Rochester?"

"He's a new teacher," Nora added, "and he's from Marblehead . . . and he drives a blue Mustang . . . and he's really handsome . . . and he's about six-foot-one . . . and he has black — "

"Whoa!" Jeff shouted, holding his free hand up. "Taste this, first." He handed each girl a teaspoon.

"Perfect," Nora said, sipping.

"Needs salt," Jennifer said.

"Salt is believed to elevate blood pressure," Nora and Jeff said together. They looked at each other and laughed.

"One health-food freak per day is enough, thank you," Jennifer said to Jeff. She tried to scowl at the big, bearlike man with the graying hair and bright blue eyes, but it came out as an affectionate smile.

Jennifer just couldn't help thinking how glad she was that he was there and how she didn't care that other people thought having a male housekeeper was weird. Jeff was the last of a long line of housekeepers Jennifer's dad had hired after his wife died when Jen and her little brother Eric were babies. But Jeff was the first housekeeper who acted and felt like a member of the family.

Nora and Jennifer threw their books on the kitchen table and sat down while Jeff returned his attention to the stove. "Now, in answer to your question about whether or not I know your teacher — " He paused dramatically, the stirring spoon poised in midair.

"Well?" Nora urged.

"Of course I do!" Jeff said, chuckling. "Cliffie's the son of my oldest buddy, Bill Rochester."

"*Cliffie?*" Nora and Jen squealed.

"Oh dear, Debby warned me not to use his childhood nickname," Jeff said. "I wonder if I slipped and said it in front of him during dinner the other night."

Nora and Jennifer's eyes grew wider. "You had *dinner* with him?" they asked in unison.

Jeff turned around. "Who do you think is responsible for Cliff's being here? Yours truly." He bowed. "See, after Cliff got his teaching credentials last spring, he had some trouble finding a job. So when I heard that the Cedar Groves School District was hiring, I went over and got him an application. The rest is history."

Jennifer flashed Nora a triumphant smile. "And you thought he wouldn't even *know* him!"

"Debby and I helped him move into his new place on Saturday and then stayed for dinner," Jeff continued. He pretended to frown. "Speaking of Debby, you two aren't the only girls who think Cliff is handsome."

"Oh, don't be so jealous," Nora teased. "Edna probably told Cliff that she thought *you* were cute."

To the girls' surprise, Jeff burst out laughing.

"Don't be so hard on yourself," Jen scolded him. "Debby knows she already has the best boyfriend in the whole world: *You*. Anyway, Cliff's too young for her." Jennifer tried to make her voice casual. "How old is he, by the way?"

"And how long has he been married to Edna?" Nora added.

The girls were puzzled when Jeff again hooted with laughter. After a minute, though, he folded his arms across his chest. "I refuse to divulge that kind of personal information about one of your teachers," he said sternly.

Jen groaned.

"Oh, come *on*," Nora pleaded.

Jeff shook his head vigorously. "Absolutely not!" But Jennifer saw him smile as he looked at his watch. "Oh, look at that. It's already four-*twenty-three*."

"He's twenty-three!" Nora and Jen screamed together.

Jeff just looked at them innocently as he crossed the kitchen to the phone. "I think I'll give Cliff a call and see how his first day went," he said, punching in a number.

Nora slapped a hand over her mouth to keep from giggling aloud and Jennifer gasped with delight.

"Hi, Cliff, it's Jeff," he said into the receiver, and the girls tried not to breathe. "So how'd it go today? Not as bad as you thought, right? . . . How's Edna? . . . Have you let her out of the house yet?"

Jennifer and Nora exchanged looks of confusion.

"Maybe you *should* let her out," Jeff continued. "Isn't that her I hear howling in the background?"

Jeff watched the girls' mouths drop open in sheer horror as they stared at each other speechlessly.

"Well, I'll check in again later this week," Jeff said hurriedly, hanging up. Within seconds, he was practically doubled over with laughter, and he went into new peals each time he looked at Nora and Jen's stricken faces. "Meow!" he finally managed to howl. "Meow, meow!"

A slow, delighted grin spread across Jennifer's face. "Edna is a *cat*!" she said with wonder.

"A big, fat Siamese cat," Jeff sputtered, dissolving into a new fit of laughter.

Nora narrowed her eyes and looked at Jen slyly. "But nobody else needs to know that, do they?" she said

The girls exchanged wicked smiles.

Chapter 3

Though Nora and Jen had seen each other only a few hours earlier, they were talking on the phone like they did every night.

"What are you wearing tomorrow?" Nora asked, trying to keep her voice casual.

"That fuzzy ski sweater my dad gave me last Christmas," Jen said, "because I . . . um . . . think he's hurt that I don't wear it much." *Cliff obviously likes blue,* is what she was thinking.

"I'm wearing my denim skirt and jacket," Nora said. "It's . . . um . . . the only thing I have that's clean." *Cliff obviously likes blue,* is what she was thinking.

Both girls were surprised by the awkward silence that followed.

"Well, I'd better go," Nora finally said. "We're out of granola, so I have to whip up another batch of my special blend."

After saying good-bye, Jen sat on her bed and picked up the blue leather diary she'd been writing in when the phone rang. Mrs. Gunter, her seventh-grade English teacher, had urged her students to keep a diary of their thoughts and dreams. Before her maternity leave, Mrs. Rickerts had also encouraged the practice. Jen suspected that Mr. Rochester would, too. Then she blushed — if he only knew what she'd written just minutes before! Flipping back a page, she read it.

Today at lunch Nora said she was "madly, totally, completely," etc. etc. "in love" with Cliff, Jen had written. *Maybe that's just Nora bubbling over, as usual. Still, she's always so sure of how she feels. She probably really does love him.*

As for me, I can't say that I love him . . . yet. All I know is that when he was talking about Wuthering Heights *in class today his whole face lit up. And I knew right then that he's the kind of person who really feels things deeply. Like me. So I was thrilled when I saw this bumpersticker on his car (nobody else seemed to notice it):* MAKE FRIENDS WITH A CAT AND YOU'VE MADE A FRIEND FOR LIFE. *Now I know what cat he's talking about! But seeing it gave me a very strong feeling that HE has very strong feelings about ALL poor, defenseless animals — not just Edna. That's why*

I've decided to give him some "Save the Whales" literature after class tomorrow and to ask him if he'd like to come to our next meeting.

Jen looked up from her diary. She decided the blue ski sweater was a good choice . . . but maybe she also ought to wear a little more eye makeup than usual, like Tracy was always bugging her to do. Besides just her normal brown mascara, maybe she ought to add a little eye shadow.

She went over and found the palette of eye shadows she'd stashed in her top dresser drawer. Tracy had talked her into buying it a few weeks ago and this was the first time Jen had even taken it out of the bag. The palette had six colors — including a blue that was almost the same shade as her ski sweater.

Jen stared at her wide hazel eyes in the long mirror over the dresser. She'd read an article about eye shadow colors in *Seventeen* a while back, but couldn't remember the rule: Were you supposed to wear eye shadow that matched your eye color or that matched what you were wearing?

Yawning, she wandered over to her closet and looked up at the *Seventeen* magazines stacked on a shelf. No way — she was too tired to page through them all in search of the article. Should she call Nora for her opinion? Or Tracy? Or maybe Denise, who was even more skilled at applying makeup than Tracy?

Jen stretched out on top of her white chenille bedspread and stared at the ceiling, thinking. Nora wouldn't be any help — all she ever wore was lip gloss. Actually, *anybody* she asked would get suspicious. She could just hear the teasing: "How come you're so interested in eye shadow all of a sudden, Jen? Does it have anything to do with third-period English?" Denise might even launch into her teacher-crush lecture again!

She sat up and grabbed her diary. *I'm not going to wear any eye shadow tomorrow*, she wrote. *Now, I'm sure I remember the article saying that your eye shadow should match your eye color. And I don't have any that's brownish-green or greenish-brown!*

She stopped for a minute and frowned. *I promised that I'd be honest with you, Diary, and I just lied*, she continued to write. *Honestly, I really don't remember what the article said. The truth is, I'm not going to wear eye shadow tomorrow because I'm afraid I won't put it on right, or that I'll wear too much, or that everyone will laugh!*

Satisfied with her decision, Jen got under the covers and turned off the light.

* * *

Nora knew it was going to be a trying day the second she stepped off the school bus and onto the sidewalk the next morning. Even from there she could see Susan and Mia standing on the school's front steps, where eighth-graders always congregated before school. Susan was wearing a royal-blue sweater and pants. And Mia's spiky hair and long fingernails almost exactly matched the color of Susan's outfit.

"Not you, too!" Susan groaned as Nora started up the steps in her own blue outfit. "I was sure you guys would all be really obvious and wear fisherman knit sweaters!"

"I don't have one," Nora said as she joined them.

Suddenly, Mia groaned, too. Nora and Susan turned to see that she'd spotted Jennifer headed their way in her bright blue ski sweater. Jen came up to them laughing nervously and twisting a lock of long black hair around her finger. She and Nora exchanged looks that were both guilty and accusing at the same time. The *real* motive behind each friend's choice of clothes was glaringly obvious this morning in the face of so much blue competition.

"Well, just be glad that we don't all sit together in English," Nora said.

Lucy Armanson, who had been talking to

Joan Wesley, overheard the remark. She turned around and peered at the group, then put a hand over her eyes to shade them. "That's for sure," she said, laughing. "Otherwise, you'd give Mr. Rochester a gigantic case of the blues." She expected the dirty look she got from Susan — but not those from all the others!

Meanwhile, Tommy Ryder strutted down the walkway that connected the junior high with the high school. He liked to walk through the high school grounds each morning to see how many of the high school girls looked at him. Today was *really* going to be his day, he was thinking. Not only had a gorgeous redhead smiled at him, she'd also said hi! And she was *at least* sixteen!

When Tommy reached the steps, he joined the girls. "Good morning, my blue angels," he said, pretending to tip a nonexistent hat.

Nora eyed him coldly. Sometimes Mr. Conceited's attempts at being suave make me gag! she thought. She was about to make a face at him when Susan shouted "There!" Four pairs of eyes followed a bright blue Mustang as it cruised slowly past the front of the school.

A fifth pair of eyes watched the girls in disbelief. So it hadn't been just a case of temporary insanity, Tommy was thinking. Yesterday, they'd gone crazy over a book, and today ... a car? I know Mitch was only joking, but maybe I am losing my touch, Tommy thought miserably, the gorgeous redhead forgotten. The girls hadn't even noticed him!

Tommy tested them. "Mrs. Peters just told me that the heating system broke down, so there won't be any school today."

Nobody even glanced at him. And nobody noticed when he stormed off.

"There's Tracy!" Nora was saying. She closed her eyes and crossed her fingers for a few seconds. "Don't be wearing blue, don't be wearing blue, don't be wearing blue," she muttered.

The girls watched Tracy hop out of her mother's car and hurry toward the steps. Everybody sighed with relief; she was wearing a pink sweater and gray pants.

"But I bet if it was warmer, she would have tried to wear a *fishnet* sweater, if such a thing existed," Susan snickered.

As Tracy got closer, the girls could see she was also wearing a large, babyish "Pokey" pin — as in "Gumby and Pokey."

Nora bit her lip to keep from laughing.

"Is that some new designer logo?" Susan asked Tracy, pointing at Pokey. "Kind of tacky for someone who usually wears an alligator or a swan."

Tracy stuck her bottom lip out in a pout. "I'm wearing Pokey for Cliff."

"Now you're going to say Heathcliff told you he was a Gumby and Pokey fan!" Susan said, rolling her eyes.

"No, but he drives a Mustang," Tracy said.

The others looked at her blankly. "Huh?" Nora said.

"Well, my mom said that a Mustang is a horse, so I figured Cliff must like horses," Tracy said, fingering Pokey.

Mr. Rochester stood very straight and still at the front of the classroom, holding an ancient-looking copy of *Wuthering Heights* open in front of him. "We crowded round, and over Miss Cathy's head I had a peep at a dirty, ragged black-haired child big enough both to walk and talk," he read aloud. "Indeed, its face looked older than Catherine's. Yet, when it was set on its feet, it only stared round, and repeated over and over again some gibberish that nobody could understand."

Suddenly, he slammed the book shut and dropped his arm to his side. There were a couple of startled gasps. "This is the boy who will grow into Heathcliff," he said quietly. "The Heathcliff whom everybody will consider to be a monster. Everybody, that is, except for Catherine and Hareton — " His fierce black eyes darted from student to student. " — And maybe you."

Mitch Pauley lowered his head to hide a yawn. This *Wuthering Heights* stuff was so confusing that he had tuned out several minutes ago when the teacher was giving a summary of the plot. What had made Mitch's head spin was that most of the guys in the book had similar, weird-sounding first names that began with an "H" — Heathcliff, Hareton, Hindley. Hindley — imagine a guy with a nerdy name like that going out for football! Mitch thought, this time smothering a laugh instead of a yawn. He'd probably be cut the first day. On the other hand, Rochester had said that the guy was a pretty mean and nasty character. You'd have to be, Mitch thought, to keep people from laughing in your face over a weird name like ... wait a minute. Had Rochester been talking about Hindley or Heathcliff? Or Hareton?

Mitch rubbed his temples and sighed. To think they were going to have to read two chapters every night and write a summary of what they'd read every week!

A spitball hit him on the cheek. Automatically, he glanced in Jason Anthony's direction. Tommy Ryder, who sat next to Mitch, also turned to see what Mitch was looking at. Jason grinned at them and nodded. Then he pointed at Nora Ryan and mouthed, "Look at that!"

Nora was staring up at the teacher with glazed eyes. She seemed to be barely breathing. After watching her for several seconds, Tommy also failed to catch her blinking. That book again, he thought irritably. It's almost like she's hypnotized by it. Suddenly, Jason threw a spitball at the back of Nora's head. It stuck in a curl.

Nora didn't move a muscle.

Jason quietly tore off a piece of notebook paper and prepared a new missile — this one jumbo-sized. It seemed to make an audible "thwoosh" sound as it sailed through the air. Jason, Mitch, and Tommy held their breaths. Bingo!

Nora didn't even flinch.

Disappointed, the boys looked around the room in hopes of at least spotting a few outraged reactions from Nora's friends. To their disgust, most of the other girls were too busy gazing at Rochester with the same stupid expression as Nora's to have noticed either hit. The power of that stupid book was incredible!

"You'll find that Heathcliff is a man torn between love and hate," Mr. Rochester was saying dramatically. "And that he can love as deeply as he can hate. Well, now, it's too bad we can't devote the whole hour to *Wuthering Heights*. But unfortunately, I'm required by law to teach you a little something about sentence structure, as well."

At the abrupt change in subject, Nora blinked several times as if she were just awakening. She watched Cliff stride to his desk to replace *Wuthering Heights* with a grammar textbook. Returning to the front of the room, the teacher opened the textbook to a bookmark. "Page 42, people," he called. Suddenly, his mouth flew open in a tremendous yawn. "Excuse me!" he said, laughing. "Guess I've got a case of the mid-morning blahs."

Nora shot straight up in her chair. He had yawned the same way and given the same excuse for it yesterday, she remembered. No healthy person should be yawning every day at ten-thirty in the morning! This was NOT just a case of the mid-morning blahs!

When the bell rang a few minutes later, Jennifer jumped out of her seat and headed for the teacher, "Save the Whales" packet in hand. Glancing behind her, she saw that Susan, Tracy, and Mia were also advancing toward him with the same determined expressions.

But Nora beat them all to it.

"Excuse me, Cli — , uh, Mr. Rochester," they heard her blurt out shakily, "but I need to know exactly what you ate for breakfast!"

Chapter 4

"Frosted flakes!" Nora said an hour later, still unable to believe it. "He eats frosted flakes for breakfast!"

Steve Crowley laughed. "You say that the same way anyone else would say, 'He eats raw hamburger with honey.'"

"It's just as revolting, if you ask me," Nora said. She handed Steve another apple to dice.

Tracy looked up from the celery stalks she and Jen were chopping on the other side of the counter. "What do you have against frosted flakes, Nora? I think they're good."

Steve grinned. "They're not just good — they're GRRRREAT!" Years of friendship with Nora and Jen made him know how to tease each of them.

"Hey, Tony the Tiger, let's have more cutting up and less cracking up over there!" called Miss Morton from the other side of the classroom. Nora could tell that the pretty young cooking teacher was trying not to smile. Everyone liked her because she was funny and good-natured . . . even when she was telling her students to shut up, like now.

"You still didn't say what you have against frosted flakes, Nora," Tracy said, her voice lowered.

Steve groaned softly. "Don't encourage her!"

"Not too technical, okay, Nora?" Jen said. "We want to be able to *eat* this Waldorf salad if we ever finish it."

"Well, for starters," Nora said, slicing a new apple in half, "frosted flakes are frosted with white death."

"White death?" Tracy asked.

"That's Nora-ese for sugar," Steve said. He slid a heap of diced apples into a large glass bowl.

"Sugar is bad enough for normal people," Nora continued. "But for someone with hypoglycemia — low blood sugar — like Cliff, it's absolute disaster. When you have low blood sugar, you feel tired and depressed. Like Cliff looks most of the time."

Jennifer took the bowl from Steve and tossed in the celery she and Tracy had chopped so far. "Nora, all he did was yawn a couple of times," she said gently.

Tracy was getting bored with the whole discussion. "I'll get the mayonnaise," she said through a yawn.

Tracy crossed the room to the supply cabinet and got a new jar. Idly, she tried to twist it open. Stuck! For a few seconds, she was annoyed. Then she suddenly remembered what had happened a few weeks ago when Jen and Nora couldn't get a jar full of egg whites open. The guys in the class had practically fallen over each other trying to get to the jar first! They all had wanted to show off how strong they were. And that cute Charlie Parker had seemed to grow two feet taller with pride after he'd finally gotten it open, and Jen had thanked him.

Tracy stood next to the supply cabinet and looked over the boys in the classroom. Who should she make feel manly today? Her eyes fell on Steve Crowley. He was *soooo* good-looking . . . tall, dark, and handsome, to be exact. How could Nora and Jennifer always be so casual when they talked to him? Why weren't they dying to go out with such a hunk? They always said they'd been buddies with him since kindergarten, but surely he looked different to them now than he had at the age of five! Were they blind or what? Well, if they don't want him, Tracy thought, heading for Steve with the mayo jar, I'll take. . . .

Cliff! Tracy stopped dead in her tracks. How could she have forgotten Cliff? If opening a stuck jar for a girl made these *boys* feel manly, imagine how manly a *man* would feel!

Cliff paced in front of the classroom with his grammar textbook open. "Words that end in 'ly' are generally adverbs," he said. "My use of the word 'generally' there is an example. Who can give me another?"

"There's a girl in the doorway frantically waving a jar of mayonnaise," someone called out.

"A weird but correct example," Cliff said, looking up from the textbook. He did a doubletake. "Oh, there really is!"

As the class laughed, Cliff made it to the door in about three long strides. He gestured for Tracy to move into the hall and then followed her.

"What's the problem . . . uh, it's Tracy, isn't it?" he asked quickly. "Is there an emergency?"

Tracy looked up at him through her long eyelashes. "Well, it's an emergency for weak little *me*," she drawled. "I can't seem to get this mean old jar open and if I don't, I won't be able to finish making my salad. And if that happens I'll get an 'F' in cooking!" She formed her lips into a pretty pout.

Cliff was staring at her. "You came all the way from the cooking lab to ask me to open a jar?"

Tracy mistook the amazement in his eyes for pride. "That's right," she said with a happy smile.

Cliff shrugged. Silently, he took the jar from her and wrenched it open.

Tracy took it out of his hands. "Oh, thank you, thank you, thank you, Mr. Rochester! You're *soooooo* strong! What would I ever do without — "

"Next time you can't get a lid off, try running it under a little hot water," Cliff interrupted, nervously glancing over his shoulder toward his classroom. "Or that's what we'll both be in if you get caught leaving class without permission."

"We'll be in hot water?" Tracy asked, her forehead crinkled with confusion.

"Trouble, Tracy," he said, edging toward the door, "we'll both be in trouble. Now get back to class before you're missed." He glanced at her Pokey pin and flashed her a dazzling smile. "And don't be pokey about it."

She had no idea he meant *don't be slow*. All she knew was that he liked Pokey and he liked her! That smile proved it.

Jennifer hurried down the main corridor after school that day hoping that she wasn't too late. Why had Mr. Armand, the French teacher, picked *her* to drop that note off in the office? The detour had cost her two minutes.

She glanced over her shoulder for the fifth time. Take it easy, Jen, she scolded. None of them are following you. Susan had left French early for a dentist's appointment. Tracy was in the cooking lab, working off a demerit for leaving class without permission. And Nora and Mia were at Drama Club, which was where Jen also would have been except that today she had the meeting at the orphanage. So, finally, she would have a minute alone with Cliff . . . if she hurried.

There he was! In another second, it would have been too late — Cliff was just about to go through the door to the teachers' parking lot.

"Mr. Rochester!" she called, breaking into a run.

He turned around, his heavy black eyebrows raised.

She stopped in front of him. "Did you get . . . get a chance to read the 'Save the Whales' literature I left . . . left on your desk this morning?" she panted.

"So you're the one who left it . . . uh . . . Jennifer, isn't it?"

Jen nodded shyly.

"Yes, I read it," he said. "And I'd really

like to come to your next meeting."

"Mr. Rochester, I hope you didn't believe the newspaper reports a couple of months ago that said all the countries signed an agreement," Jen blurted out. "What actually happened was . . . you'll *what*?" Her voice broke.

"I'll come to the next meeting," Cliff said, laughing. "I'm new in town, so I'd like to get involved in some activities. This sounds like something I could get behind."

Jennifer was speechless.

"Well," Cliff said, touching his head in a sort of salute, "I'll see you tomorrow night at the meeting."

As he went out the door, Jennifer was still too stunned to remind him that he'd also see Jennifer Mann, the luckiest girl in the world, in class tomorrow!

Tommy Ryder and Mitch Pauley were hurrying along another corridor toward the auditorium. Neither wanted to be late for Drama Club because Mrs. Hogan sometimes made latecomers do embarrassing improvisations. A few weeks ago, for example, she'd made Mitch — the captain of the football team — get up on stage and pretend to be a baby taking his first steps. He could feel his ears turning red even now, just remembering it.

Suddenly, they were cut off by a redhead

on wheels. Jason Anthony jumped off his skateboard and held his hands up, as if to physically stop the boys. "News flash: Those girls aren't in love with the guy in the book. They're in love with Rochester."

Mitch and Tommy laughed. "Yeah, and I'm in love with your great-grandmother," Tommy said. He and Mitch went around Jason and kept walking.

Jason tagged along behind them. "Wait! I'm serious. Didn't you notice the way they kept giving him those mucky looks this morning — I mean, even *after* he stopped talking about *Wuthering Heights*?"

"Well, they were probably still all weirded-out over the book, that's all," Tommy said.

"Look, Anthony, we've gotta go," Mitch said. "If I were you, I'd keep my weird theories to myself. Or they'll lock you up and throw away the key." He laughed. "Rochester!" he said, reaching for the door-knob.

"Wait, I have more proof," Jason said quickly. "This afternoon, in history, I heard Tracy blabbering to Denise about how strong and handsome *Cliff* looked when he opened her jar of mayonnaise, and how that made her crazier than ever about him. Well, excuse me, but unless we happen to be in the twilight zone, book characters do not open jars for us."

Mitch and Tommy exchanged looks and Mitch pointed to his ear and made the circular "he's crazy" gesture.

"You *are* in the twilight zone," Tommy said to Jason. "What would Tracy be doing in English with a mayonnaise jar?"

Without waiting for an answer, Mitch and Tommy slipped through the auditorium door. Oh, terrific! Everyone was seated and Mrs. Hogan was at the podium. They were late.

A wicked smile spread across Mrs. Hogan's face. "Ah, Mr. Pauley, Mr. Ryder — we've been waiting for you! I'd like both of you to go up on stage and pretend to be pieces of bacon in a pan under which the flame has just been turned on high!"

That evening, Nora stood on a stepladder looking through the stacks of cookbooks and cooking magazines on top of the refrigerator. After a few minutes, she turned and looked down at her mother, who was sitting at the kitchen table. Jessica Ryan was a Legal Aid attorney and, as was the case almost every evening, the table was covered with open law books.

"Mom, have you seen the cookbook Aunt Billie gave me for Christmas last year?" Nora asked.

Mrs. Ryan put her finger on a page to mark her place and looked up at her daughter with a blank expression on her face.

"You know, the one where all the recipes are sugar-free, salt-free, fat-free, or all three," Nora said.

"Oh, right, the one that *should* be called the '*No Fun At All Cookbook*,' " Mrs. Ryan said, laughing. "It's up there somewhere. Look inside that big *Betty Crocker* binder. It might have gotten pushed in there by mistake."

It had. "Got it!" Nora said, climbing down.

Nora's older sister Sally wandered into the kitchen. As usual, she was wearing a leotard, tights, and leg warmers. "Oh, no!" she groaned when she saw the cookbook in Nora's hand. "You're not going to bake that awful bread again, are you? That stuff that tasted like a sponge made of sawdust?"

"I am not baking tonight," Nora said loftily. "But for your information, that bread is about the healthiest food ever invented. It contained not one iota of salt, sugar, or fat."

"It was also inedible," Sally said, heading for the refrigerator. "Even Dad said so, and he's usually your bravest guinea pig."

"Speaking of guinea pigs, Sinbad loved that bread," Mrs. Ryan said, winking at Nora.

"Sinbad's a hamster, Mom," Nora said.

"Whatever he is," her mom said, "he ate every bit of it."

Sally laughed. "Remind me to thank him." She poured a glass of milk.

"I thought you had to cram for a history midterm tonight," Mrs. Ryan said to Sally.

"I do," Sally replied, closing the refrigerator.

"Then how come I hear thumping and loud music every time I walk past your room?"

"I always study better if I exercise first," Sally said. With a glass of milk in one hand and an apple in the other, she managed to pirouette before dancing out of the room.

Even though Sally had made the cracks about the bread, Nora couldn't help glancing after her sister sympathetically. A student at the nearby university carrying the standard load of freshman courses, what Sally *really* wanted was to become a professional dancer.

"What *are* you doing with that cookbook?" Mrs. Ryan asked Nora.

"Well, one of my teachers is obviously hypoglycemic — "

"That's the low blood sugar thing, right?"

Nora nodded. "Anyway, I'm putting together a new diet for him. It'll be really

47

high in protein and low in sugar and other concentrated carbohydrates. This book has a couple of good sugarless recipes. I thought I'd throw them in, too."

Mrs. Ryan looked surprised. "The *teacher* came to you for nutritional advice?"

Nora laughed nervously. "Well, Mom, he didn't exactly ask me to do this. I'm just going to *suggest* it."

Mrs. Ryan looked like she wanted to say something, but she didn't. Instead, she returned her attention to the law book.

"He'll feel one-hundred percent better," Nora said, more to convince herself than her mother. What she was thinking was, Do I really have the nerve to hand a teacher a diet? One that demands that he change his whole eating life?

Nora took a shaky breath, held her head high, and started for her room with the cookbook. Sure she had the nerve! After all, this diet would completely change Cliff's life for the better. It would make him happier and more energetic than he'd ever dreamed possible. And who would he have to thank for that? Who, among all the others, would he like the best?

As if to confirm the answer to that question, Nora heard Bruce Springsteen singing "She's the One" as she passed by Sally's door.

I will be the one, Nora thought gleefully.

Chapter 5

A few mornings later, Susan Hillard stood just inside the door that led to the teachers' parking lot. She glanced at her watch for the third time: two minutes to go. "Heathcliff" always came through that door at exactly seven-forty-five.

Angrily, Susan remembered how Nora, Jennifer, Mia, and Tracy had all tagged along when she had walked Heathcliff to his car the afternoon before. Fortunately, Susan thought, I'm the only one of us smart enough to think of meeting Heathcliff before school. Or was it, Susan wondered, that she was the only one brave enough? After all, most eighth-graders wouldn't be caught dead inside the building before the first bell rang. Well, they can just freeze to death out on the steps, for all I care, she thought, as she nervously fluffed up her thin, straight bangs with her fingers. Heathcliff is more important than what other people think.

And anyway — Susan took a fast, smug glance around — who was going to see her? This little-used corridor was deserted.

Susan felt a cold blast of air as the door swung open. She whirled around and pretended to be reading a bulletin board that got so little attention it still featured a faded Halloween dance poster.

"Oh, I'd say I'm getting about twenty-seven miles to the gallon."

It was Heathcliff!

"That's not bad for city driving," Mr. Armand replied.

Darn! For the third morning in a row, Heathcliff wasn't alone. Yesterday, it had been Miss Morton. Why do they all have to pull into the parking lot at the same time? Susan thought irritably.

Another cold blast announced a new group of teachers and a couple of their kids who were students at the school. Susan was relieved; now she could discreetly follow Heathcliff. Walking on the fringe of the second group, Susan tried to tune out their conversations so she could hear Heathcliff and Mr. Armand.

"How's Edna?" Mr. Armand asked.

Thrilled, Susan crept a little closer. She was about to hear more details about Heathcliff's wife!

Heathcliff shook his head sadly and held

up his left hand. Susan saw a long, angry-looking scratch.

Mr. Armand whistled. "That's quite a gash, Cliff."

"It's Edna's way of letting me know how much she hates it here," Heathcliff said grimly.

Susan stopped dead in her tracks, unaware of the laughing, chattering teachers around her. Mouth hanging open, she stared after Heathcliff in disbelief.

In English later that morning, Nora snuck her third look at Cliff while keeping her head bent over her notebook. He was providing class time for everybody to work on their written *Wuthering Heights* summaries. But Nora was too nervous and excited about giving him the new diet to concentrate. Instead, she was writing *Nora Rochester*, *Nora Ryan-Rochester*, and *Dr. Nora Ryan-Rochester* over and over again in print so tiny that she was sure the girl next to her would need binoculars to read it.

Nora followed Cliff with her eyes as he crossed the room from his desk to the window. He stood looking out, lost in thought. She loved the tweed jacket he was wearing over his fisherman knit sweater. It had a lot of green in it. She glanced down at her forest-green sweater dress. They'd look so good standing next to each other! Nora sighed — they'd look even better if she weren't so short.

Restlessly, she tapped her pen on the paper. After class, he'd be surrounded by girls, as usual. Would she have time to do more than thrust the diet into his hands before someone else claimed his attention?

One minute before the bell, Mia got up and went to the pencil sharpener, holding a few albums under her arm. Nora was furious — now Mia was a lot closer to Cliff at the window than she was. Nora looked around for something *she* could logically do that would put her closer to Cliff. But there was nothing.

The bell rang. Nora jumped out of her chair and rushed forward. She was delighted to see that Mia, on a similar course, had crashed into Tommy Ryder. That delay put Nora in the lead.

"Mr. Rochester!" she gasped, sailing the diet into his hands. "Your fatigue is probably the result of hypoglycemia."

Cliff nodded a little and swallowed. "The . . . uh — "

"Mr. Rochester! I brought you a couple more albums!" Mia waved at him. "I think you'll like Throbbing Gristle — "

"It's a low-blood-sugar disorder," Nora interrupted.

"It is not!" Mia snapped. "Throbbing

52

Gristle is an English punk band that broke up a few years ago, unfortunately. But Black Flag, here, is — "

Cliff's head was swiveling back and forth between Nora and Mia.

Nora glared at Mia. "I'm talking about hypoglycemia!" She turned to Cliff. "It happens when your sugar-regulating mechanism goes haywire, and the only way to treat it is with this kind of diet." She pointed at the papers in his hands.

Suddenly, Tracy stepped right in front of Nora. "Oh, Mr. Rochester . . . could you pull the cap off this mean old pen? Pretty please? It's on too tight for weak little me!"

"Did you see that Mia gave Heathcliff *more* punk albums today?" Susan asked Nora and Jennifer a few hours later. "He's going to have sore muscles if he ever tries to carry that pile."

Nora nodded and rubbed her arms, which were covered with goosebumps. It was always so cold in the gym, and being forced to wear shorts didn't help. "Why is Mia being so dense about it?" Nora asked. "I mean, he obviously isn't taking them home to listen to them."

"She told me he listens to them right in the classroom during lunch some days," Jennifer whispered. She hoped Mia, who was talking with Denise not far away, couldn't hear them. "And Susan, Mia isn't *giving* them to Cliff. She told me she's just lending them."

"She'd better not give them to him," Nora said. "Every one of them was a gift to her from Andy."

Susan's eyes gleamed. "Really? That's interesting news. Next time I see Andy, I think I'll ask him if he knows where his precious gifts are these days. By the way. . . ." Susan stopped and thought for a few seconds. "Oh, never mind." She wandered away.

Nora rubbed her hands together, still freezing. Much as she hated the daily aerobics workouts, today she almost wished they could get started. "I need a warm-up to warm up," she muttered to Jen.

Jennifer flashed her a sympathetic smile. It was considered uncool to so much as flex your fingers before Mrs. Scott appeared on the scene. Jen glanced at the clock that was protected by a wire cage high up one wall. Three more minutes. Like a true drill sergeant, Mrs. Scott was never late. "By the way," Jen said to Nora, "you didn't tell me you already finished your *Wuthering Heights* report. Isn't that what I saw you handing to Cliff after class?"

Nora laughed nervously and ran a hand through her curly brown hair. "No, that was a diet."

54

Jen groaned. "Oh, Nora, you didn't."

"Yes, I did! I explained what hypoglycemia was, and he nodded and seemed really interested . . . and kind of touched."

Jennifer shook her head. "I watched when you were talking to him, Nora. And to tell you the truth, I thought he looked sort of *confused* or something."

"Well, I had to make it a pretty quick explanation," Nora said irritably. "I mean, Mia kept trying to barge in, waving those albums she brought in his face."

Susan came up behind them and cleared her throat. "You guys, I. . . ." Nora and Jen turned to her. Susan shook her head and closed her mouth. Then opened it. Then closed it.

"What is it, Susan?" Nora asked.

Oh, why not? Susan asked herself. I can't keep this to myself any longer. "You guys, this morning I heard Heathcliff tell Mr. Armand the most awful thing. He showed Mr. Armand this really bad scratch on his hand. Then he said his wife attacked him, just because she hates living in Cedar Groves!"

Jennifer bit her lip hard. She dared not look at Nora.

Nora was nodding, a serious expression on her face. "Yes, we did hear from Jeff that Edna's been a problem," Nora said when Susan finished. "He says Cliff has to keep Edna locked up all day and that she just howls."

Susan nodded slightly, her features frozen in shock. Jen bent down to tie an already tied lace, terrified that Susan would see how she had to twist her face to keep from laughing.

"Jeff told us that when Cliff comes home, he lets Edna go outside for a few minutes," Nora went on solemnly, "but that he has to watch her every second or she'll run away."

Susan backed away from Nora and Jennifer, her face still frozen, her eyes wide.

Just then, Mrs. Scott marched in blowing her whistle. "Two lines of ten!" she barked. "On the double!"

Jennifer and Nora scurried into place. "That was cruel!" Jen mouthed to Nora. "You just broke her heart." She finally allowed herself a torrent of giggles under cover of Mrs. Scott's repeated whistle blasts.

Nora grinned back at Jen. "One less girl to compete with. Now we only have to worry about Mia and Tracy."

And each other, they both thought, exchanging sly but guilty looks.

"Just keep talking, Ryan and Mann, if you want to be doing laps during lunch!" Mrs. Scott bellowed.

Nora and Jen immediately clamped their mouths closed. The teacher called roll.

"Hillard?"

"Here?" Susan murmured faintly. It sounded like a question. Again, Nora and Jen couldn't look at each other for fear of bursting into loud laughter.

A few minutes later, the Pointer Sisters' "Neutron Dance" was bouncing off the gym walls.

"I want to see some sweat!" Mrs. Scott hollered, almost drowning out the sisters.

Susan usually hated aerobics as much as Nora did. But today, she barely felt herself doing the kicks and jumps and bends. Heathcliff has an insane wife he must keep locked away just as Edward Rochester was forced to do in *Jane Eyre*, she kept thinking. How tragic! How horrifying!

And how utterly romantic!

After school that day, Tommy Ryder leaned against a wall and waited for Denise Hendrix to come out of the girls' room. Thirty feet away, one foot on his skateboard, Jason pretended to be engrossed in *Wuthering Heights*. But every thirty seconds or so, he would look up, catch Tommy's eye, and nod encouragingly.

Denise finally came through the door, snapping the clasp of her Gucci purse.

"What's your hurry, beautiful?" Tommy asked, blocking her.

"Would you mind?" Denise said irritably. "I'm meeting Timothy Marks and I'm already late."

Normally, that remark would have made Tommy jealous. But today, all he felt was relief that she didn't just wander past him in an unhearing fog. Or run past him, as if he were invisible, shouting to another girl about a parking lot. Or about a Mustang. Or about a book character who was more of a J.R. Ewing than a Prince Charming, from what Tommy had read so far. Finally, a girl in her right mind! Just the kind he needed to talk to. "That's okay," he said to Denise, "I'll walk along with you."

And to Denise's extreme annoyance, he did. Even worse, Denise glanced behind her and saw that creepy Jason Anthony was tagging along right behind them on his skateboard.

She stopped and faced Tommy with a sigh. "What do you want?" Better get rid of them before Tim, absolutely the best-looking guy in the whole school, saw her with jerky guys like these! Strangely, though, Tommy seemed to be at a loss for words. That was a first!

He opened his mouth and then clamped it shut. How did I let Jason talk me into asking her? he thought. Not only is it a ridiculous question, no matter how I phrase it, it'll be admitting that I, Tommy Ryder, am actually having a problem with girls!

"He wants to know if the other girls have a crush on Rochester," Jason finally said.

Denise groaned and rolled her eyes. "Yes! And I am so glad I had to make up a test during lunch today. I was afraid I'd scream if I heard one more gushy word about Cliff Rochester."

Jason gave Tommy a triumphant smile. "What'd I tell ya?"

Tommy was still speechless, only this time it was out of shock. Denise turned and walked away. Tommy hurried after her and finally got his mouth unstuck. "Is there anything we can do?" he asked miserably.

Denise tossed a lock of shiny blonde hair over her shoulder. "Absolutely nothing," she said. "You'll have to let it burn out on its own. And that will happen sooner or later, I promise. Let's hope it's sooner."

She heaved a world-weary sigh. "How many more schoolgirl crushes will I have to endure?" she asked the ceiling. "Well, everyone has to learn on her own." She faced Tommy and Jason again. "Listen, all you can really do right now is ignore the situation and pretend everything's normal. Whatever you do, don't let them hear you making fun of Mr. Rochester or putting him down. That'll just backfire. It will only make them feel more protective of him."

Denise glanced at the gold bracelet watch she'd bought in Switzerland. "I'm so late! Now *good-bye*." She hurried off.

"Wait a minute!" Tommy called after her angrily. "We can't just act like nothing's happening! They don't even notice us as it is! That's *crummy* advice!"

Denise whirled around, but continued to walk backward. "Well, *excuse* me for not being Ann Landers! But I'm telling you, she'd probably say the same thing! Go ahead and ask her!" She disappeared around a corner.

A girl passing by accidentally dropped a book on the floor and Jason attempted to make a tight circle around it on his skateboard. "Should we?" he asked Tommy.

"What?"

"Should we write to Ann Landers?"

"Nope — it would take too long to get an answer," Tommy said absently. "But I think I do have a plan. Let's find Mitch and Andy and talk it over."

At eight-thirty that evening, Susan dropped her pen, rubbed her eyes, and re-adjusted her desk lamp. Yawning, she re-read the last sentence she'd written: *In Chapter 7, Catherine finally returns to Wuthering Heights after staying at*

Thrushcross Grange for five weeks.

If she was this bored reading just her own summary, she could imagine how bored poor Heathcliff would be having to read twenty-five of them! And hers wouldn't stand out at all, she just knew it. Oh, sure, she'd taken great pains to make her handwriting perfect. And she'd tried to utilize big words, like "utilize," whenever possible. But her summary would still be just about the same as everybody else's. What could she expect when everybody was reading the same story? She crashed her fist down on the desk in frustration.

As if on cue, Van Halen's "Why Can't This Be Love?" blasted through the wall from the room next door.

Susan stood up and pounded on the wall. "Turn it down!" she shouted.

"Sorry, but I can't hear you!" her sixteen-year-old sister Kelly shouted back.

Very funny, Susan thought irritably, flopping down on her bed. Kelly knew Susan hated heavy metal. And Susan knew Kelly wasn't that hot on it herself — she just had this one album that someone had given her as a gift.

So she's punishing me, Susan thought, but for what? Was it because I called her Jelly Belly Kelly when she took the last brownie? Or was it because I said her new boyfriend looks like a cross between Fred

Flintstone and the Pillsbury Doughboy?

Susan smiled wryly. Sometimes, figuring out *why* people did what they did was more interesting than what they actually. . . .

She sat bolt upright. That was it! That was how to stand out from all the others! She wouldn't just tell what happened in *Wuthering Heights*, she'd also try to explain *why*. She'd pull apart each character's personality, search for motives in their childhoods, act like a psychologist! She thought of poor Heathcliff at home, forced to baby-sit an insane wife. He would be so fascinated by her theories . . . and so impressed!

She seized her pen.

It was after eleven when Susan finally put the pen down. Sleepy but satisfied, she reread the last two sentences of her five-page paper. *Because of the cruelty that was inflicted upon him as a child, it is part of Heathcliff's personality to enjoy watching his enemies destroy themselves, as Hindley begins to do in Chapter Eight. Meanwhile, though she is becoming more arrogant and haughty every day, Heathcliff loves Susan all the more.*

Susan caught her breath. She had written *Susan* instead of *Catherine*! Was it just a slip of the pen? Or was it — Susan hugged herself — *an omen*?

Chapter 6

The following Tuesday morning, Cliff moved slowly among the desks, passing back the freshly graded *Wuthering Heights* reports. "Everyone should have read Chapter Ten by now," he said. "So who can tell me why Edgar is upset about Isabella's crush on Heathcliff, his rival from across the moors?"

Several hands shot up. "Tracy?" Cliff said, sounding a little surprised.

Tracy put her hand down. "What's a moor?"

Susan turned around in her seat and glared at Tracy. She had already explained "moors" to the girls! Susan couldn't resist. "What's a moron?" she muttered under her breath. Several people around her laughed.

Cliff defined "moors," then glanced at his watch. "I guess we'd better leave *Wuthering Heights* and move on to sentence construction. Keeping in mind yesterday's discussion, who can give me a sentence that contains both an adverb and an adjective? Wait — let's make it tougher: a sentence that has *two* of each."

Jennifer waved her hand.

"Go for it, Jennifer," Cliff said.

Jennifer threw a split-second sly look Nora's way and struggled to keep from smiling. "Slowly and carefully, I bit into the rich, flaky donut."

Cliff groaned. "Oh, don't torture me! Nora here has forbidden my eating — " He broke off and scowled at Nora. "Am I allowed to even *say* the word, Nora? Nora here has forbidden my eating *donuts* and everything else that's remotely edible!"

Susan and Mia sat up straight and turned to Nora with smug, triumphant smiles. Nora bent her head, bit her lip, and felt tears stinging behind her eyes.

"On the other hand," Cliff continued, sending a dazzling smile at Nora, "I thank her for her thoughtfulness."

Nora raised her head and beamed.

When the bell rang a few minutes later, she was in such high spirits that she practically skipped down the aisle.

Jennifer was waiting for her in the hall. I'm not going to let her gloat, Jen vowed as a smiling Nora came closer. "Did I tell you that he smiled at me *twice* at last week's 'Whales' meeting?" she asked before Nora could open her mouth.

"You told me three times," Nora said cheerfully. She glanced at Jen as they headed for their lockers and was thrilled to discover she was only a tiny bit shorter than Jen when Jen wore her Reebok running shoes while she wore her gray leather boots. What a day this was turning out to be!

"Well, maybe I didn't make it clear," Jen was saying. "I mean, he smiled at me *during the meeting*, when everyone was supposed to be paying attention to the speaker."

"You told me three times," Nora repeated. "But while we're on the subject, I don't think it's fair of you to ask Cliff to devote so much time to the whales right now. I mean, changing to a new diet is stressful on the body, so he's probably still having bouts of fatigue. At least give him a few weeks to get adjusted."

Jennifer gave her a sweet, innocent smile. "Oh, don't worry about him, Nora. He can keep up his strength with the Coke and cookies people always bring to those meetings."

At lunch, Susan, too, was determined not to let Nora rub it in about her small victory. Susan marched up to the girls' usual cafeteria table carrying a bowl of pudding and waving her *Wuthering Heights* paper.

"Pass it around!" she ordered. "But don't spill any food on it. I'm going to frame it."

Jennifer took it from her. *Brilliant!* Cliff had written at the top in his large, strongly slanted hand. *You have managed to get to the core of what makes these characters tick. This is college-level work.*

"*Wow,*" Jennifer said, unable to keep a note of envy out of her tone. She handed the paper to Nora, who read it and passed it on to Tracy.

Susan smiled smugly. "It's obvious that Heathcliff prefers the intellectual among us."

Tracy, moving her lips, slowly read Cliff's comments. She looked up when she finished. "You're wrong, Susan. I think men like girls who make *them* look smart."

"Is that what you're trying to do, Tracy?" Susan sneered. "Well, let me tell you, questions like the one you asked today don't make him look smart, they make *you* look dumb! And anyway, a man who likes *Jane Eyre* isn't going to go for Jane Air-head." She laughed merrily.

As Tracy was about to reply, Jason sailed by the table with his nose in the air. He didn't even look at the girls. Denise was right behind him with her tray.

"That's funny," Jennifer said, moving her chair over to make room for Denise at the table. "Wonder why Jason didn't stop to bug us, as usual?"

The next person to pass the table was Tommy, wearing his usual "I-know-you-can't-resist-me" smile. He stopped. "Hello, *Denise*," he said, as if she were alone.

Then it was Jason again, stomping past, loudly clearing his throat.

"What's going on?" Nora asked.

Denise suddenly remembered the conversation she'd had with Tommy the week before. "Well, it seems pretty obvious that they've decided not to pay any attention to you because you haven't been paying any attention to *them*," Denise said.

Susan snorted. "They sure are going out of their way to show us that they're not paying any attention to us!"

Jennifer turned to Denise. "You mean, they're upset because of — "

"Don't say his name!" Denise groaned, putting her hands over her ears. "Can we have just five minutes where the name C-L-I-F-F isn't mentioned?" She dropped her hands with a sigh. "But, yes — I'd say these guys are punishing you."

"You call this *punishment*?" Susan asked, pointing at Jason as he walked silently past the table for the third time. "I love it! And I hope it lasts. No more of

Jason's paws in our pudding. We don't have to worry about him contaminating everything with cooties."

"*Cooties*?" Jennifer said, giggling. "I haven't heard that word since third grade!"

Susan's face reddened.

Nora held up her grapefruit juice in a toast to Susan. "Here's to the intellectual among us!"

After school that day, Tracy redid her lip gloss with precision and a tissue. "Here comes Andy, with Mitch and Tommy," she whispered, watching in the mirror she'd taped inside her locker door. "Didn't you say you wanted to talk to Andy, Susan?"

Susan closed her own locker and turned around casually. "Hey, Andy! You must be the one giving all those albums to Mr. Rochester. That's really nice of you," she said sweetly.

To her surprise, the boys walked right by without a word, without even a glance her way.

"I'm talking about punk albums, Andy!" Susan yelled after them, wondering if Andy just hadn't heard. "*Thirty* punk albums, to be exact!"

The boys didn't even turn around. They soon turned a corner and went out of sight.

"I didn't think they were going to keep

this up," Susan said. "And I didn't figure Andy would be in on it, either."

"In on what?" Tracy asked.

"This so-called *punishment*."

Tracy looked confused. "You mean they're punishing us now, too? Besides just ignoring us?"

Susan sighed with exasperation. "What a space cadet! Where were you at lunch when we discussed this?"

"I was thinking about Cliff," Tracy said, pouting. Suddenly, her eyes widened. "That reminds me — we better hurry or Nora and Jen will have Cliff all to themselves on the way to his car."

"Don't sweat it," Susan said. "Nora told me at lunch that she had to go straight home if she ever wanted to memorize her lines for that scene she and Mitch are doing for Drama Club. And didn't Jennifer say this is the day she does her thing at the old peoples' home?"

Tracy nodded, relaxing a little.

Suddenly, the two glanced at each other, panicked. "Mia!" they said in unison, and took off, running for the teachers' parking lot.

Meanwhile, around the corner up ahead, Tommy was holding one of Andy's arms, Mitch was holding the other, and Andy was struggling to break free. "Let me go! I've gotta go back and ask Susan what she meant by that crack! We can make *one* exception, can't we? Just this once!"

"No!" Tommy shouted. "No exceptions, or Operation ST will fail. When I said silent treatment, I meant the *complete and total* silent treatment. Not one word! And no pantomiming either, remember? No nodding at them, or shaking your head. Those are talking, too."

Mitch let go of Andy's arm and straightened his letter sweater. "And no waving hello or good-bye, right?"

"Right," Tommy said. "Complete silence. Until they see reason. Otherwise, they'll be hanging around this Cliff forever. The Cliff Hangers."

Mitch laughed. *"The Cliff Hangers.* I love it."

"Well, I hate it, man," Andy said, then he sighed. "You're sure this'll work?"

"It'll work," Tommy said firmly.

"I just better not find out that Mia's giving that guy *my* albums," Andy grumbled. "Because it sure sounds like that's — "

"What'd I tell you?" Tommy interrupted, nudging him, as Susan and Tracy flew around the corner. "Do I know women or what? Here they come, just dying to find out why we aren't speaking to them. Remember: Operation ST! Let's stick with it, even if they beg us. Even if they promise not to say one more word about you-know-who. Let's just let 'em suffer for a few more days. As punishment."

The boys made a great show of deliberately turning their backs on the rapidly approaching girls.

The girls ran by so fast that this time they didn't even notice they were being ignored.

At seven-thirty that evening, Mia Stevens was sitting cross-legged on her bedroom floor listening to a Violent Femmes album and painting her fingernails. She'd already painted half of each nail white and was now doing the other half in black. Mia hated to be a copycat, but she'd fallen in love with this black-and-white effect when she'd seen Exene Cervenka's nails on a recent MTV interview. At least Exene hadn't done a similar number on her lips, as Mia was planning to do tomorrow morning. She was even thinking of dying her hair that way, if she had the time tonight.

"Mia?" her father shouted from the bottom of the stairs.

Mia lowered the volume on her stereo with her big toe. "I already loaded the dishwasher, Daddy!"

"Andy's here!"

Surprised, Mia turned the stereo off and headed for the stairs, waving the hand with the wettest nails. Andy hadn't said anything at lunch about coming over. Wait a minute . . . she hadn't seen him at lunch. She'd been hanging around outside Cliff's classroom, hoping he'd come back from lunch early to listen to one of the albums she'd brought him. He hadn't today, but yesterday she'd had five whole uninterrupted minutes of Cliff . . . and the Raunch Hands.

When Mia walked into the living room, Andy handed her a flat, foil-wrapped package and headed for the front door without a word.

Mia ran after him and turned him around. "Andy?"

He looked right through her, his face expressionless.

"You're mad at me?" Mia asked. "Then why am I getting a present?"

No reaction.

"Well, then, why am I getting the silent treatment?"

He turned his back again and made for the door.

Mia was suddenly inspired with an idea. "Toad says he saw you buying a Michael Jackson album yesterday."

Andy whirled around with a horrified expression. Mia burst out laughing.

"Well, is it true?" she demanded. "Are you really going Top-Forty on me?"

Andy gritted his teeth. He wanted to shout "No! No! Toad's a liar!" or "You're making that up, Mia!" or to at least shake his head. But Tommy had said that shaking your head, nodding, even waving goodbye were considered talking, and therefore in violation of Operation ST. Andy turned on his heel and stormed out the front door.

"Then you don't deny it!" Mia called after him, laughing merrily. "Andrew Warwick, I am shocked! Wait'll everyone hears about *this*!"

Still laughing, she unwrapped the package on her way back up the stairs. The new Trilogy album she'd been wanting! Mia was tempted to slit the cellophane with a fingernail and get the record on her turntable right away. But she managed to control herself and to put it, unopened, with her school books. She and Cliff should inaugurate new albums together!

Two blocks away, Jennifer was stretched across her bed on her stomach with her head hanging over the side. She was holding the phone with one hand and brushing her long black hair with the other.

"Have you memorized your lines — eighty-six — for that scene you and Mitch are doing — eighty-seven — tomorrow?" she asked.

"Jen, it's an old wives' tale that you

should brush your hair a hundred strokes a night," Nora said on the other end of the line. "It just makes your hair greasier faster."

"I don't care — ninety-four. It feels good."

"Anyway, yes, I've got my lines memorized," Nora said. "I hope Mitch does, too. I asked him about it in biology today, but he just ignored me."

Jennifer laughed. "I think this silent treatment thing is kind of funny."

"Really," Nora said, yawning. "As if we cared. Such *childish* behavior — but it fits. They just seem like such *babies* since we met Cliff, don't you think?"

"Mmm-hmm," Jennifer said. She rolled off the bed and put the brush on the dresser. "Do you think anyone in the entire Drama Club picked the word *love*, Nora?" Jen asked.

At last week's meeting, Mrs. Hogan had divided the club into boy-girl couples and handed out a list of one-word emotions. The assignment was to write and perform a scene of dialogue that showed this emotion. Nora and Mitch had chosen "nervousness"; Jennifer and her partner, Randy Phillips, had picked "confusion" and would perform next week.

"No. But I sure would have if Cliff had been my partner," Nora said.

"Are you nervous about tomorrow?" Jennifer asked.

Nora laughed. "Yes. But Mitch and I are *supposed* to be acting out 'nervousness,' remember? No one except you will know that I'm not acting! How about you? Think you'll have stage fright next week?"

Jennifer sighed. "I don't know. At least Randy and I are going to have time to rehearse ours. Too bad you and Mitch have to go first. But I guess somebody has to."

"It's my fault," Nora said. "I'm the one who pulled the date out of the hat."

"Well, just remember that I'll be rehearsing with Randy in the auditorium during lunch on Friday," Jennifer said. "Jeff's making me a sandwich to bring. He asked me if I wanted to bring one for Randy, too. Can you believe that? No way! Randy would get the wrong idea."

"Jennifer's got a boyfriend!" Nora sang.

"Nor-a! He's at least three inches shorter than me. That's why when we wrote the scene, I suggested that it take place in a car. That way we'll be sitting, get it? Pretty clever of me, if I do say so myself."

Nora laughed. "Pretty *sneaky*. Don't you wish all males were as tall as Cliff?"

Jennifer sighed. "I wish all males were Cliff, *period*."

Chapter 7

Steve Crowley tapped the egg with a knife and broke it cleanly in two. With an air of expertise, he quickly transferred the yolk back and forth from half-shell to half-shell, letting the white drip into a bowl below. Finally, nothing remained in the shell but the yolk. Steve then managed to deposit it in a separate bowl with one hand while neatly tossing the shells into a garbage can halfway across the cooking classroom with the other.

"Hold your applause, please," he said haughtily to Jennifer and Nora. "The chef must not be distracted during the delicate process of separation."

Jennifer clapped anyway. Nora didn't look up from the script she was studying.

Steve pointed with his knife at the two remaining eggs on the counter. "All right, you guys, who's next?" He picked up one of them and pretended that it was shaking. "Now, now, steady there, my good man," Steve said. "This won't hurt a bit." He let loose a wicked laugh.

Nora looked up at the tall boy with a sigh. "Stee-eeve, could you hold it down a little?"

Steve's voice took on a high, squealing pitch. "No! Please! Please don't separate us! My yolk is all I've got!"

"Shut up, you!" Steve talked back to the egg in a gangster accent. "Or I'll make meringue outta ya!"

"What a performance!" Nora said, exasperated. "If mine is half as good this afternoon, I'll be happy."

"Good-bye, cruel world!" Steve said in his egg voice. He cracked it open with the knife, grunting like a TV cowboy does when he's been shot in the stomach.

A few counters away, Miss Morton looked up. "Are you making meringue or a movie, Mr. Crowley?" she called.

"I'm performing an egg-secution," he replied.

The entire class groaned.

Miss Morton headed their way.

"Thanks a lot, Steve," Nora grumbled. She quickly folded her script and thrust it in a drawer in the cooking counter.

The teacher watched Steve separate the final egg. "You do have a certain flair for this, Steve," she said. "I can't do much better myself."

He ducked his head modestly and plucked at the sleeve of his red plaid flannel shirt. "When your dad owns a restaurant, you learn to do this before you learn to say 'Mama.'"

Nora wished Miss Morton would leave. She wanted to go over her lines just one more time. Finally, someone across the room called for Miss Morton's help.

"I never thought this many people would show up," Nora said, the second the teacher was out of earshot. "We really have a lot of competition."

Steve ran a hand through his thick dark hair. "*What* are you talking about?"

Jennifer giggled. "Those are her first two lines in the scene she's doing with Mitch in Drama Club this afternoon."

Steve wiped his hands on his apron and took out the script Nora had stashed in the drawer. "I'll do Mitch's lines," he said. He peered at the page. "Most of these kids — "

"That's *my* line," Nora snapped. "Look, if you really want to help, just keep quiet and let me study on my own, okay?"

"Boy, are you touchy!" Steve said with an offended air.

As she measured out a half-teaspoon of vanilla, Jen's big hazel eyes filled with sympathy for both of them. "Steve, Nora's just upset because she doesn't know how well Mitch knows *his* lines," she explained.

"Those guys are still giving you the silent treatment?" Steve asked.

Jen nodded. She turned to Nora. "And Nora, I bet he has his lines down cold, just like you do! I'm sure he doesn't want to make Mrs. Hogan mad. You know how embarrassed most of the guys get when she makes them do those crazy improvisations as punishment."

Steve snorted with laughter as he handed Nora the bowl and the portable electric mixer. "Mr. Pauley!" he said, in a very good imitation of Mrs. Hogan. "As punishment for flubbing two of your lines, I want you to portray an egg white as it interacts with an electric mixer!" After a fast glance to make sure Miss Morton's back was turned, Steve jumped up and down, arms flailing, eyes wild. Jennifer cracked up.

"I'll volunteer to be the beaters," Nora muttered, snapping them into the mixer and turning it on full blast.

Wearing lazy grins, Mitch and Tommy sauntered down the auditorium aisle. Most of the other Drama Club members stood talking in small groups, but Jennifer and Nora were already seated in the third row. Jen was quietly reading aloud each of

Mitch's lines, so that Nora could reply with her own.

Mrs. Hogan swept down the aisle toward the podium, clapping her hands. "Let's get started, people. I believe Mr. Pauley and Miss Ryan are scheduled to perform today."

Ever the jock, Mitch leaped up the stairs to the stage and went backstage to collect the two chairs they needed.

Nora stood up and brushed nonexistent crumbs from the front of her red corduroy skirt. Why hadn't she worn pants today? she chided herself as she made her way up the stairs. Now everyone would see her knees quaking!

She went to the center of the massive stage. "Our scene is called 'The Audition,'" she announced in a quavering voice as Mitch set the chairs up.

Nora and Mitch sat down and Nora began nervously tapping one foot, as she'd planned. "I never thought this many people would show up," she began shakily. (Was she glad they'd picked "nervousness"!) "We really have a lot of competition!"

Mitch was supposed to say, "Don't sweat it. It's only a commercial for a new spearmint gum. It won't be the end of the world if we don't get it." But he didn't. What seemed like a whole minute dragged by.

Mitch said nothing, just slumped down further in his chair, made himself comfortable by crossing his long legs, and threw a sidewise smirk in Nora's direction.

Oh, no! she screamed inwardly. She'd worried about him not knowing the script by heart, not projecting his voice, or not putting any expression into his lines. But not this! She was *totally* unprepared for this! There was dead silence for what Nora was sure was at least another minute. Frantically, she ad-libbed: "I know it's only a commercial for a new spearmint gum, but I want it so bad!" Then she went on to her next real line: "Most of these kids look so much older than we do . . . so much more experienced and calm!" she wailed. "First-timers like us will come off looking like hicks!"

Mitch was supposed to say, "Stop worrying! The ad said the producer wants a brother-sister pair in their early teens. So most of these people will be cut right away for being too old." But he didn't. He just stuck his nose in the air and stubbornly folded his arms across his chest.

Nora was again forced to add his lines to her own so that the audience would be able to follow the story. "I know the ad called for brother-sister pairs in their early teens and that that'll disqualify most of these people." She took a deep, shaky breath and went on to her next regular line: "But look at that pretty girl over there!" She pointed to her left. "She looks about thirteen, and I just saw her in an Esprit sportswear commercial. And that boy there. . . ." Nora pointed in front of her. "He seems about the right age, too, and I've seen him a million times in Pepsi commercials. I'm sure they'll pick people like those two — people with familiar faces!"

This time, Nora didn't even wait for the silent treatment. She immediately adapted Mitch's next line for herself. "Yes, I know the ad said they wanted *unknowns*, but. . . ." Nora stopped. To her horror, she couldn't remember her next line. The strain of trying to do both his lines *and* hers had left her mind completely blank. Panicking, she struggled to at least remember the plot. Maybe that would help . . . oh, yes! The scene was supposed to show Nora making a very calm Mitch increasingly nervous with all of her observations, while ironically, she finally calms down thanks to Mitch's soothing remarks.

But remembering the plot didn't help. She was still drawing a blank. Desperately but discreetly, she appealed to Mitch for help by kicking him with her formerly tapping toe.

He turned to face her, giving her nothing but a slow, maddening grin.

Suddenly, something in Nora snapped. Jumping up from her chair, she faced him, shaking a fist. "How could I let you get me into this?" she shouted, the script forgotten. "I refuse to let you make a fool out of me any longer!"

Mitch just kept grinning, comically holding his hands in front of his face, as if he physically feared this girl who was little more than half his size. Nora heard male laughter from the audience. That made her even angrier.

"Say something, you coward!" she practically screamed at Mitch, stamping her foot.

Still grinning, he simply swiveled around in his chair, turning his back to her.

"All right then, you mean, horrible, despicable worm!" Nora shouted. "All right then! YOU ARE ON YOUR OWN!" She turned on her heel and stormed across the stage and behind the curtain where she burst into tears.

The next thing she heard was thunderous applause and Mrs. Hogan calling "Bravo! Bravo! Nora, come out and take a bow!"

In shock, Nora wiped her face on the curtain and tottered out to center stage, where a bewildered-looking Mitch was standing with his hands in his pockets. For a split second, Nora thought everyone was making fun of them. Then she remembered that almost no one — including the teacher — had seen their script or had even known which emotion she and Mitch had chosen.

Mrs. Hogan was still clapping. "Nora, your anger was *extremely* convincing. And Mitch . . . Mitch! What a brilliant portrayal of the strong, silent type!" She faced the class. "People, you have just seen proof of how one facial expression can be worth a thousand words!"

Nora took a deep bow, delighted.

"If any other team in this class picked 'anger,' they've got a tough act to follow!" Mrs. Hogan continued.

Mitch shook his head. "But that wasn't the emotion we — " Nora cut him off with a sharp elbow jab in the stomach. *"Now* is the time to keep your mouth shut," she hissed without moving her smiling lips.

Mitch shrugged and left the stage. He threw himself into the chair next to Tommy's. Nora sailed past them. "Thank you *so* much, Mitch," she said sweetly, her brown eyes twinkling. "Thanks to you, I'm a star!"

There was a sudden loud clap of thunder outside and several people jumped. "What was that?" someone called.

"That," Tommy muttered to Mitch, "was the sound of Operation ST falling flat on its face."

Chapter 8

At five minutes of eight that evening, Jennifer was sitting in another auditorium, this one connected to the Cedar Groves Public Library. She was happy to see that it was filling up fast and that there were many new faces. This might be the best turnout yet for Cedar Groves' Save the Whales Association.

When the clock on the wall clicked to seven fifty-eight, Jennifer turned halfway around in her seat so she could see the door at the back out of the corner of her eye. She didn't want to look *too* obvious. Still, her heart beat faster knowing that *he* would walk through that door at any second. Cliff was never late, but he always came in at the last possible minute. He jogged in the evenings, he'd explained to her at last week's meeting, and needed to shower before showing up. Jennifer hadn't told the other girls about Cliff's jogging.

Not even Nora. Having a little bit of knowledge about Cliff that no one else did made her feel kind of special.

Seven-fifty-nine. Jennifer tapped her fingers nervously on the giant "Save the Whales" pin she was wearing. Where was he?

Eight o'clock. Conrad Matthews, the bald, elflike little man who was president of the organization, went to the podium.

"Welcome, friends, whether this is your first time with us or your hundredth," he said into the microphone. Though that was his usual jovial opening, he seemed sad. "Unfortunately, it's my unhappy duty to report to you a bad situation that's developed off the coast of Peru, thanks to a large corporation with no heart."

Jennifer bit her lip. Half of her listened and felt like crying as Conrad described how a company's fishing operations were accidentally killing whales. The other half worried about Cliff. Had he been in an accident? Gotten sick? Or maybe, Jen thought, he just doesn't care about the whales anymore. Or about me.

Suddenly, the door creaked open loudly. Jennifer and a number of others automatically turned around. Cliff! He stood in the doorway, red-faced. Jennifer caught his eye, then caught her breath. His whole face had lit up when he saw her!

She was astonished to see him start walking down the center aisle. He wasn't going to take a seat in the back, like the other latecomers did! He wanted to be closer to her!

At the podium, Conrad was emotionally reading a letter he had sent to the president of the Peruvian fishing company.

Cliff stopped at Jen's aisle. The aisle seat was vacant, but Cliff slid past it . . . past one person . . . two . . . three, four. . . . "Ouch!" the fifth person cried.

"Sorry," Cliff mumbled.

Six . . . seven. Jennifer couldn't believe it. He was causing this big distraction, he was going through all this embarrassment, just to sit next to *her*!

He dropped into the empty seat beside her. "Ran out of gas!" he whispered.

Jennifer couldn't say anything. Jennifer couldn't even breathe. But she did know exactly what she'd later say to her diary: *Tonight Cliff proved how much he likes me.*

At that same moment, Nora was straightening the picture frames on her dresser for the tenth time that evening. Then she flopped on her bed and stared at the ceiling. Her homework was finished and it was too early for bed. She felt restless, she felt like talking to someone . . . but who? Jen would still be at her weekly whales meeting. With Cliff! Nora thought, feeling a stab of jealousy.

Suddenly, she sat up and reached for the phone on her nightstand. She'd call Steve and let him know that everything had turned out just fine in Drama Club. After all, she'd been kind of rotten to him in cooking.

Within seconds, she was giving Steve a complete blow-by-blow of the afternoon's events.

Steve laughed when she finished. "What a relief! You turned what could have been a disaster into a hit!"

Nora sighed. "Yeah."

"You don't sound too happy about it. Are those guys still giving you a hard time?"

Nora laughed. "You mean those *children*? Hardly. It's just that . . . well, I just feel really *frustrated* about something, that's all."

"About what? Come on, you can tell Uncle Steve."

Nora paused and thought for a minute: Why not? Steve is a male, after all. Maybe he can give me some pointers.

"Well, you know how a bunch of us sort of have a thing for Cliff," she said slowly.

"I'd have to be deaf, blind, living on Jupiter, or all of the above not to," Steve said.

"Anyway, I'm pretty sure he likes me." Nora described how she had developed the new diet for the teacher and how he had praised her for it.

"It *does* sound like he likes you," Steve said. "So what's the problem?"

"But Steve, he likes *everybody*. *That's* the problem. He goes out of his way to smile at Jen at whales meetings. He compliments Susan about her *Wuthering Heights* papers. He seems to love Mia's punk albums. I think he even finds Tracy sort of amusing." She took a deep breath. "Steve . . . I want to make him like *me* the best. But how?"

There was silence on Steve's end of the line.

"Steve? Come on, help me out. You ought to have a couple of good ideas. After all, you're a man, too."

"Aw, Nora, hey," Steve said. Nora could almost *hear* him blushing! "Look, give me a few minutes to think about it, okay? I'll call you right back."

Steve hung up the phone, hoping that he had sounded confident. Actually, he was petrified. "Why me?" he groaned out loud. What does she think I am? he thought. Some kind of expert on getting the attention of the opposite sex? Me, Steve Crowley, the guy who has trouble getting up the nerve to even smile at most girls? Why doesn't she ask someone like Tommy Ryder who attracts girls without even trying . . . or at least thinks he does?

Then Steve remembered: Tommy and a bunch of the other guys weren't speaking to Nora and the girls.

He tipped his desk chair back and stared at the ceiling. What other guy could he send Nora to for advice? Jim Blake? Charlie Bernard?

Steve slowly lowered the front legs of his chair to the floor with a sigh: He'd have to come up with some advice for her on his own. Definitely. After all, she'd called him a man! If he didn't come up with *something* . . . well, that made him just a dumb kid, didn't it? And he didn't want anyone thinking that about him — not even Nora, who, like Jen, had been a buddy for practically his whole life.

He stood up and began pacing his room and racking his brain.

Steve had said he'd call right back, but it was almost ten when the phone rang at the Ryan home. In bed and half asleep, Nora picked up the receiver and heard Steve asking Sally if he could speak to her.

"I've got it, Sal," Nora said sleepily.

"N-G-A-B!" Sally sang. It was the sneaky, secret-code way of saying "Nora's got a boyfriend!" Nora guessed she deserved it: Last year, when she was in seventh grade, she had sung "S-G-A-B!" whenever a boy called Sally.

"It's only Steve, Sally," Nora said irritably.

"Oh, hi there, Steve!" Sally said. "Didn't recognize your voice. How ya doin'?"

Steve and Sally chatted for a minute. Twice, Nora cleared her throat loudly and meaningfully. Finally, Sally hung up.

"Well?" Nora asked.

"Well, I gave this a lot of serious thought," Steve said. "And I was about to give up. I mean, absolutely nothing was coming to me. But then I came down to the kitchen for a snack and that's when it hit me — double-fudge chocolate cake!"

"A double-fudge chocolate cake hit you?"

Steve sighed impatiently. "No, dummy, didn't I ever tell you the story about how my mom snared my dad? That's *her* word for it, by the way."

"I don't think I've ever heard that one."

"Okay, then listen," Steve said, his mouth full. He was obviously eating some of the cake for inspiration. "Once upon a time, my dad was the most popular guy on campus. Every pretty girl in the college was interested in him, including my mom. She says she tried everything to make him notice her — different perfumes, new hairstyles, crazy clothes. Nothing worked. UN-

TIL the day she brought him a piece of her double-fudge chocolate cake for lunch. One bite . . . and he was hooked. Of course, my dad says it was Mom, not the cake." Steve whispered the last sentence.

Nora sighed with disappointment. "I can't bring Cliff any of your mom's double-fudge cake, dumb-dumb! I've got him on a sugarless diet!"

"All right, but you can bring him some other kind of food to go bananas over, right? To put it more accurately, you need to impress him with your cooking skill. Your *culinary talent*, as we say in the biz."

"You may be right," Nora said thoughtfully. "There's no time to make anything tonight. But I could whip up something tomorrow night and take it to him Friday. And tonight I could at least. . . ." Her voice faded away.

"There are a million different things you could spring on him," Steve said. "Like how about that lemon-baked chicken you're always bragging about? Or your herbed green beans?"

Nora didn't respond.

"Nora?"

The receiver lay on her bed. She was racing downstairs, once again in search of what her mother called *The No Fun At All Cookbook*.

Chapter 9

Jennifer rushed into English before the bell the next morning with shining eyes and cheeks flushed with cold. As she headed for Nora's desk, Nora thought she looked prettier than ever. Her pink and white coloring was further heightened today by the bright red sweater she was wearing with her black stirrup pants.

"Have I got news for you!" Jen said.

"No cavities, right?" Nora asked. Jennifer had missed her first two classes because of a dentist's appointment.

"Right! But this is even better. Are you ready for this? Last night, Cliff sat next to me at the whales meeting. Not only that, he had to climb over about a hundred pairs of legs to do it. And there were a bunch of empty seats easier to get to. But he wanted to be by *me*!"

Nora faked a yawn. "*That's* the big

news?" she asked, striving for a so-what? tone.

"Oh, Nora, I could hardly breathe the whole time! I mean, I could smell his after-shave. He wears Aramis, like my dad. And I could see the hair on his arm!"

"Whoopdy-doo."

"I suppose *your* evening was equally as thrilling," Jennifer snapped.

"Actually," Nora said, "I had a very interesting conversation with — " She stopped suddenly. What are you doing, Nora? she chided herself. Why should you tell her what Steve suggested? If Cliff went through so much trouble to sit next to her, he might already like her better than you! Why give her even more of a head start?

". . . I had a very interesting conversation with Sally about her biology homework," Nora finished weakly.

"Is that all?" Jen asked, and she didn't have to fake her so-what tone.

Three aisles away, Tommy Ryder opened his binder to a clean sheet of notebook paper. "CLIFF ROCHESTER" he wrote at the top, curling his left hand around it so that nobody would see what he was doing.

The bell rang as Cliff entered the room and headed for the front. As students scurried for their desks, Tommy studied the teacher, then picked up his pen. *Wears a fisherman knit sweater almost every day,* Tommy wrote.

"A lot of you seemed to have a problem with Chapter Nine in your latest *Wuthering Heights* summaries, so I'd like to devote a significant amount of time to that this morning," Cliff said.

Tommy wrote again: *Doesn't seem to spend much time combing his hair.*

Cliff paced in front of the class, holding open his personal copy of *Wuthering Heights.* "Chapter Nine is one of the most significant chapters in the book. It shows the tight bond that exists between Catherine and Heathcliff. On the other hand, she also betrays him here by marrying Edgar—"

Tommy added to his list: *Uses the words "significant" and "on the other hand" A LOT!*

Cliff aimed a dazzling smile at Susan. "As our own Susan Hillard so brilliantly boiled it down, this chapter clearly exposes the two violently conflicting sides of Catherine's personality." The other girls refused to give Susan the satisfaction of a jealous glance. But Susan didn't care. She was thinking, *I just died and went to heaven.*

And Tommy was writing: *Shows EVERY ONE of his teeth when he smiles.*

When the bell rang forty-five minutes later, Tommy stood up and turned to Mitch across the aisle. "What are you doing after school?"

Mitch shrugged. "No practice today."

"What do you say a bunch of us guys get together at Temptations?" Tommy asked. "I've been doing a lot of thinking about the Cliff Hangers, and I've — "

Mitch scowled as he put on his letter sweater. "If you're going to ask us to keep up Operation ST, count me out." He nodded toward Cliff, who was surrounded by five chattering girls. "It obviously didn't work."

"No, this is a new plan and it's much better," Tommy said. "I *guarantee* this one will work."

Mitch's face brightened. "Three-thirty?"

"Three-thirty." Tommy smiled mysteriously.

At lunch that day, Mia Stevens stood inside the cafeteria, near the door, fuming. First Cliff had made that sappy remark about Susan's paper. Now, on top of that, he'd gone into the teachers' dining room late, which usually meant he wouldn't leave early to listen to one of her albums. Mia calculated the distance between the teachers' dining room, herself, and the table where the other girls were sitting. If Cliff *did* come out early, at least she would get to him first.

Suddenly, Andy appeared at her side. "Long time no see," he said. "Or I guess it should be long time no speak to."

"Yeah," Mia said, uninterested.

Andy stood next to her in silence for several minutes, trying to think of what to say. He couldn't even catch Mia's eye.

"Want to eat lunch together?" Andy finally asked.

"I already ate," Mia snapped. "And I'm busy."

Andy stormed away.

Steve Crowley, eating a sack lunch with some of his friends at a nearby table, had seen Mia and Andy standing together but couldn't hear what they were saying. He was surprised when Andy stomped away from Mia. To his even greater surprise, he saw that Mia was gesturing at him to join her with a long, sky-blue fingernail. Steve slid a plastic-wrapped piece of his mother's double-fudge cake into his knapsack to eat later and went over to Mia.

"Steve, I'm desperate for male advice," she said, "and I think you're the guy to get it from. Nora and Jen always talk about how helpful you are. Will you help me?"

Steve nodded, puzzled. "I'll try."

"Okay, here goes," Mia said. "How can

I re-interest somebody who seems to be losing interest?"

Steve stared at her. Andy didn't look like he was losing interest, he was thinking. He just looked mad. You don't get mad at someone you're not interested in. He opened his mouth to say it aloud, but changed his mind. I guess she should know better than I do how Andy feels about her, he thought. Maybe he has lost interest.

"It just so happens that I do have an idea," Steve said, last night's conversation with Nora fresh in his mind. "Are you any good at cooking, Mia?"

Meanwhile, halfway across the cafeteria at a large center table, Denise Hendrix was going into her fifteenth minute of describing the country club dinner-dance that Timothy Marks had taken her to the weekend before.

Jennifer pretended to be listening, but she was actually thinking about Cliff and feeling depressed. Here she'd been sure he'd tried to prove his feelings for her at the meeting last night. What a commotion he'd made, just to sit next to her! She'd gone home and devoted a whole page in her diary to the scene. But today, he hadn't made eye contact with her during English. Not even once. He hadn't even glanced in her direction, in fact! He seemed to like

Susan better. Or was he just fickle — liking one girl one day and another the next? Well, she couldn't stand that. She wanted him to like *her* all of the time. But how could she get him to do that?

Jennifer caught sight of Steve Crowley talking with Mia. Maybe what I need is help from another guy, she thought suddenly. And Steve is the perfect guy to get it from! I've known him forever, so I won't feel embarrassed about asking or have to worry about what to say next. And he sure has been more of a friend lately than most of the other guys, with their silent treatment and other childish behavior!

Jen watched as Mia waved at Steve and left the cafeteria. Steve headed back to his table. Jennifer stood up abruptly, right in the middle of one of Denise's sentences.

"Where are you going?" Nora asked.

Jennifer glanced down at her. "Uh . . . to talk to Steve."

Nora narrowed her eyes. "About what?"

"About something I didn't understand in biology," Jennifer mumbled, avoiding Nora's eyes.

"Then *I'm* the one to ask," Nora said, surprised. But Jennifer had already left the table. She's hiding something from me and I don't like it one bit, Nora thought irritably as she watched Steve get up from his table and follow Jen to a corner of the cafeteria. Then, with a stab of guilt, Nora remembered how she'd withheld her own conversation with Steve from Jennifer just that morning. Is this any way for best friends to treat each other? she asked herself, shifting uncomfortably in her chair.

Meanwhile, all the color was draining from Steve's face as he listened to what Jennifer wanted. Well, Crowley, you've really got yourself into a mess this time! he thought. Go ahead — try to come up with different advice for Jen than you gave Nora! And what would happen if the new advice worked better? Nora would kill you, that's what! And if what you told Nora worked better, it'd be Jen on your case.

Steve sighed. "Well, Jen, have I ever told you the story about my mother and my dad?"

As Steve filled Jennifer in, neither was aware that Tracy — across the room, pretending to listen to Denise — was staring at them, her mouth set in a thoughtful little "O."

After school that day, Tracy dashed down the main corridor in search of Steve. She found him leaning against his locker, eating the cake he had saved from lunch. "Steve!" Tracy said breathlessly. She batted her eyelashes while gazing up at him as if he were ten feet tall. "I need some manly advice."

Steve wondered whether someone had stenciled ANN LANDERS on the back of his jacket. He didn't even wait for Tracy to ask. "The way to a man's heart is through his stomach," he boomed heartily.

Susan Hillard, passing by, pretended that she hadn't heard. Obviously, she thought excitedly, Tracy brought some cake for Steve. That means she's finally over Heathcliff! Hooray! One down, three to go.

Susan went to her locker, opened it, and continued to sneak peeks at Tracy and Steve from behind her locker door. Before Heathcliff had arrived on the scene, Susan remembered, Tracy had spent a lot of time sighing about how good-looking Steve was and complaining about how he never paid any attention to her. Now, the way Steve had his head bent close to Tracy's, he seemed pretty taken with her all of a sudden. Just because she'd brought him a piece of cake? Well, Susan thought, it must be just as Steve himself had said — the way to a man's heart *is* through his stomach!

Thanks, Steve, Susan said silently. And then she slammed her locker and dashed from the building.

She passed Temptations a few minutes later, but she was in such a hurry to get home that she didn't even glance in the window. So she didn't see Tommy, Mitch, Jason, and Andy spooning down hot fudge sundaes at the big front table.

Andy caught sight of Susan rushing by outside. "There goes Susan. *Cliffie* must be all tucked in his blue Mustang," he said sarcastically.

Mitch threw his spoon into his empty sundae glass. "I bet if we had cars, they never would have even looked at that skinny old guy," he said bitterly.

"At least *I* have wheels," Jason said, gesturing at his skateboard, which the manager had made him leave by the door.

Nobody laughed.

"When I'm sixteen, I bet my dad will buy me a car," Mitch said. "Especially if I'm the star of the high school football team. But I'm not settling for a Mustang. I'm gonna get an old Porsche and put a turbo-charger on it."

"And a chrome exhaust," Jason added excitedly.

"And paint the whole car black," Andy said.

Mitch snorted. "I'll make old Rochester look like he's driving a little toy wagon!"

Tommy banged on the side of his sundae dish with his spoon to get their attention. A frown creased his good-looking face. "Come on, you guys, let's get down to business here. I've done a lot of thinking, and it finally hit me that there's only one way to prove to those girls that Rochester isn't so special." Standing up, Tommy took some three-by-five index cards from the back pocket of his jeans and passed them out to the others.

"What are these?" Andy asked.

"Your instructions," Tommy replied. "Now, there isn't anything we can do about the car, but. . . ." He let his voice trail off as he watched the boys read the cards.

Jason looked up and nodded thoughtfully. "I see what you mean."

Andy was also nodding, convinced. "Is there a code name for this one? You know, like we had Operation ST before."

"Hmmm," Tommy said, leaning back in his chair to think. "I guess if we *have* to have a code name, it could be Operation I.Y.C.B.H.J.H."

Mitch shook his head. "I'll never remember that."

Tommy laughed. "Well, even a dumb jock like you can remember what it stands for: If you can't beat him, join him!"

Chapter 10

Nora's sister Sally came sniffing into the Ryan kitchen that night. "Mmmm! What's cooking?"

Nora closed *The No Fun At All Cookbook* and climbed up the stepladder to return it to the top of the refrigerator. "Zucchini casserole," she said.

"I can't believe it," Sally said, sitting down at the kitchen table. "Something from *that* cookbook actually smells good."

Nora gathered up zucchini, onion, and carrot peels from the chopping block and threw them into the sink. Then she remembered to set the timer over the oven for forty minutes.

"What's it for?" Sally asked, holding her thick dark hair on top of her head. "Are you guys throwing a potluck at lunch tomorrow? Or is it for a boyfriend?" Sally was only teasing, so she was surprised to see Nora's face go bright red.

Nora quickly turned her back on Sally, though she was sure Sally had seen her blush. She switched on the garbage disposal and waited for her sister to sing out "N-G-A-B!" But it was Nora's turn to be surprised.

"So it *is* for a boy," Sally said gently. "That's nothing to be embarrassed about, Nora."

Nora still couldn't turn around. "You don't think it's dumb?" she mumbled, pretending to be busy at the sink.

"No, I don't." Sally paused. "But if you want my honest opinion, I don't think you should have made a zucchini casserole," she said in the same gentle tone. "I know how you feel about sugar and all, but if I were you I'd just grit my teeth for once and present this boy with a handful of cookies."

"It's not — " Nora hesitated and then sighed. Well, why not confide in Sally? she asked herself. Nora turned around and faced her sister. "It's not for a boy my age," she said. "It's for a teacher — Cliff Rochester. A new English teacher." She waited for an explosion of laughter from Sally.

Sally didn't even crack a smile. "Oh," was all she said.

Nora nodded toward the oven. "Think he'll like me more for bringing it to him?" she asked quickly, before she lost her nerve.

"If it tastes as good as it smells, he will," Sally said. "You know, I had a crush on a teacher when I was in eighth grade, too."

"Mine's not a *crush*."

Sally didn't hear her. "Mine was on my Italian teacher — Salvatore Mario. Is he still there?"

Nora bit her lip hard to keep from bursting out laughing. After all, Sally hadn't laughed at her. But *Mr. Mario*? "He's my homeroom teacher," Nora finally managed to say, with a straight face. "Didn't I tell you that?"

To her surprise, Sally dissolved into laughter, dropping her leg to the floor with a loud thump. "Oh, Nora!" she sputtered. "When I had him, he had just come back from two years of study in Rome." She stopped laughing and took a deep breath. "He had this romantic little accent when he spoke English, and he wore Italian sweaters and Italian sandals with socks. He just looked so *different* from all the other men ... so ... so ... what's the word? *Continental*. So dashing!"

Sally went over to the cookie jar, took out a pinch of Nora's homemade granola, and popped it into her mouth. "We were reading *Romeo and Juliet* in my English class that year, and I used to substitute 'Salvatore' for Romeo and 'Sally' for Juliet!" She began to howl with laughter again. "Oh, Nora, last summer I saw him at Safeway and barely recognized him!"

She headed for the doorway, wiping her eyes and laughing helplessly. "Someday, little sister, you'll be laughing about Biff, too."

"It's *Cliff*!" Nora yelled after her. "And I'll *never* laugh at him."

But Sally didn't hear her. She was climbing the stairs and shouting "Salvatore, Salvatore, wherefore art thou, Salvatore?"

Before school the next morning, Nora marched down the main corridor ignoring the weird looks she was getting from various seventh-graders and pretending that people lugged three-quart Corning Ware casseroles to school every day.

She was just about to turn the corner into the corridor that led to the teachers' parking lot when she heard the shouting.

"How dare you steal my idea!" That was Susan.

"*Your* idea? This was *my* idea — and it was pretty crummy of you to steal it and fix yours on the same day!" That was Mia.

Nora's heart sank. As she rounded the corner, her fear was confirmed. Susan, Mia, and Tracy each held a box that obviously contained food.

There was a collective groan as they, in turn, caught sight of Nora's dish.

"Oh, shut up!" Nora said irritably. She set the casserole on the floor. "If I'd known everybody else was going to play Suzy Homemaker, I sure wouldn't have!"

"At least this Suzy Homemaker didn't *make* hers." The girls turned around to find a very disappointed-looking Jennifer. She was carrying a box of candy with a sticker that read "Thanks for your support. All candy funds go to aid South American earthquake victims."

Nora glared at her. Had Steve given Jen the food idea, too? He wouldn't dare, Nora thought. Maybe last night, when Jen had phoned after Sally and Nora's conversation, Sally had given the idea away by saying something like "I'll call Nora — she's down in the kitchen cooking a dish to bring to Biff." Yeah, that was probably it. But that didn't explain how the rest of them had had the same idea at the same time. Had Jen told them? Uh-uh. Why would she do that when it would spoil her own effort?

"I had this idea first!" Tracy said. "I thought of it yesterday right after school. So it's only fair that the rest of you take your food home and bring it back another day."

Nora stamped her foot. "For your information, I thought of doing this Wednesday night."

"Big deal. I thought of it last week," Susan lied.

"Then why didn't you bring something last week?" Mia jeered.

"Because . . . um . . . our oven was broken!" Susan said. "Now you people just go put your stuff in your lockers and ——"

Jennifer clapped her hands. "You guys, stop it! Do you want to be fighting when Cliff comes in? Why don't we just agree that . . . well, as Nora said not too long ago, great minds think alike."

Each girl abruptly closed her mouth. No one wanted to admit the thought that occurred to all of them — it didn't come from *my* great mind, it came from *Steve's*!

"And anyway," Jen finally continued, "we obviously didn't all bring the same thing. *That* would have been embarrassing." She turned to Mia. "What are 'Meat Puppets,' by the way?"

Everyone looked at the Chinese takeout box, complete with a handle, that Mia was holding. She had decorated it with zebra stripes and painted "The Meat Puppets" across the front in purple nail polish. It matched her outfit.

Mia sniffed. "The Meat Puppets just happen to be one of the best groups in the entire world. I thought I would sort of honor them by naming these Swedish meatballs I fixed for Cliff after them."

Nora shook a finger at Jen. "How could you bring him candy, you traitor? You might as well have brought him a gun! Sugar is just about as good for him!"

"Oh, Nora, face it," Jen said with a sigh. "The man has to eat sugar once in a while. He's only human."

"She's right, Nora," Susan chimed in. She held the bakery box she was carrying up to Nora's eye level. "For your information, I put two whole tablespoons of your dreaded white death into these scones!"

"What are scones?" Tracy asked.

"English biscuits," Susan said loftily. "The British adore them at teatime. I bet Heathcliff — the one in the book, I mean — ate them by the dozen."

Jennifer giggled. "I think The Scones sounds like a better name for a punk group than The Meat Puppets."

Susan peered at the card Nora had taped to the cover of her dish. "Well, Nora, what bland, tasteless, but no doubt totally healthy creation are you forcing on poor Heathcliff?"

"Zucchini casserole," Nora snapped. "And as the card says, it's very high in protein while containing not one granule of refined sugar or flour. If you're interested, I've listed every single ingredient, down to the pinch of garlic powder."

Susan pointed at the right side of the card. "What are all these numbers?"

"Those are my estimates of the amount of protein, thiamine, riboflavin, iron, and calcium per serving — and how those amounts compare to the U.S. R.D.A. That's *recommended daily allowances* to you amateurs."

Susan lost interest and switched her attention to Tracy, who had opened the shoe box she was holding and was counting the contents. Susan moved closer, looked into the box, then pretended to jump back in fear. "What are they?" she shrieked.

"Sugar cookies," Tracy said.

"I guess the question should have been how *old* are they?" Susan said. "They're covered with mold!"

"No, they're not!" Tracy said hotly. She held the box out so that the others could see the cookies. "I just added some blue food coloring to the dough. I mean, I got to thinking last night: Since Cliff has a blue Mustang, blue must be his favorite color!"

Suddenly, the door opened at the other end of the corridor. Cliff came through the doorway, his dark head haloed by the early morning sunlight.

"He's alone!" Tracy squealed.

"No, he isn't," Susan grumbled. "Look, there's Mr. Carpenter right behind him."

Nora held her curly brown head high.

"Now, since we're all going to go through with this, let's just wait here for him calmly, like adults," she said sedately. But she was the first to break away from the group and bound down the corridor, shouting "Mr. Rochester! Mr. Rochester!"

Jennifer, with her much longer legs, soon overtook Nora, with Tracy and Susan right behind her. Mia was in last place, thanks to her three-inch spike heels.

Cliff came to a dead halt and stared at the advancing girls. When Jennifer reached him, she practically threw her candy at him. He was forced to drop his briefcase to catch the box.

"I brought you some chocolate-covered caramels," Jennifer said breathlessly.

"Snickerdoodles," Tracy gasped, thrusting her box on top of Jennifer's.

"Scones!" Susan's box went on the pile.

Mia had overtaken Nora. "The Meat Puppets!" she cried.

A split-second later, Nora was trying to wedge the big casserole dish between Mia's punked-out Chinese takeout box and Cliff's chin.

"But girls, my birthday isn't until May ninth!" Cliff wailed. The Corning Ware dish slid precariously. "John!" he shouted to Mr. Carpenter. "Help me!"

But the history teacher was laughing too hard to be of any help.

Chapter 11

The mood at lunch that day was glum.

Tracy sighed. "Cliff seemed kind of upset when we all handed the food to him this morning, don't you think?"

"Not upset," Nora said, swallowing a bite of carrot. "I think he was just surprised . . . *overwhelmed* maybe."

Susan shook her head. "He was just plain *embarrassed*. Everything would have been fine if Mr. Carpenter hadn't stood there laughing. Why can't Heathcliff just *once* come in from the parking lot alone?" she asked irritably.

"*I* felt embarrassed when he made that crack about how his birthday wasn't until May," Nora said, neglecting to mention the exact date, as the teacher had. (She hoped the other girls had forgotten. Little did she know that they, too, had rushed to write "May 9th" in their notebooks as soon as possible.) "I mean, I wouldn't think of giving a zucchini casserole as a birthday gift."

"More like a book about the nutritional properties of zucchini, right?" Susan asked.

"Yeah," Nora said, missing the sarcasm.

"Where's Jennifer?" Tracy asked her.

Nora gestured toward the door with her carrot. "She's in the auditorium practicing her Drama Club scene with — " Suddenly, she clamped a hand over her mouth to muffle a burst of laughter.

Tracy and Susan whirled around to see what she was looking at. Tommy, Mitch, Jason, and Andy stood talking not fifteen feet away. And every one of them was wearing a fisherman knit sweater.

"I *thought* there was something different about those guys today," Susan said, laughing with Nora. "I just didn't figure it out till now, when I can see them all together."

Tracy giggled. "Do you suppose they're starting a Cliff fan club?"

"Actually, I bet this is just another move to get us to quit *ours*," Susan said.

Tracy's smile turned into a pout. "You started a fan club for Cliff and didn't ask me to join?"

"It's just an expression, Tracy," Susan said, exasperated. "There *is* no club." She glanced back at the boys. "As if they could look even *half* as good as Heathcliff does in that kind of sweater," she said disdainfully. "Well, I'm not impressed. I'm *insulted.*"

Nora was still laughing, practically doubled over. "Look . . . at Andy!" she gasped. "He . . . had . . . to . . . go . . . punk even . . . in . . . that . . . preppie . . . sweater!"

Tracy and Susan again snuck peeks in the boys' direction. Then they, too, hid explosions of laughter behind their hands. Andy was wearing a studded collar and had his hair done up in its usual spikes. He also had threaded several soda can poptops into the yarn of the front of his sweater in a snakelike design.

"They're laughing!" Mitch whispered to Tommy.

"But not at us," Tommy insisted. "I don't think they've even seen us yet." He cleared his throat noisily. "On the other hand, I think it's significant that Catherine's health does improve with Edgar's help in Chapter Thirteen," he said loudly.

Jason coughed and nodded. "On the other hand," he practically shouted, "it's also significant that, even though her health improves, Catherine doesn't want to live."

The girls didn't hear either remark. Before Tommy had even opened his mouth,

Nora had noticed the label on the back of Jason's sweater. That sent her into new peals of uncontrollable mirth. "You . . . aren't . . . going . . . to . . . believe . . . this!" she gasped to Susan and Tracy. "JASON . . . IS . . . WEARING . . . HIS . . . SWEATER . . . INSIDE . . . OUT!"

The girls were still laughing when the bell rang.

Tommy, Mitch, Andy, and Jason made their way out of the cafeteria.

"Are you *sure* they weren't laughing at us?" Mitch asked Tommy.

Tommy drew himself up to his full height. "Yes, I'm sure. Girls don't laugh at Tommy Ryder."

"Then what were they laughing at?" Andy demanded.

"Who knows with girls?" Tommy said. "Maybe they were telling food jokes."

Mitch scowled as the boys headed for their lockers. "It doesn't matter what they were doing," he said. "What matters is that they still aren't paying any attention to us. Maybe you're not as much of an expert on girls as you think, Ryder. Maybe this plan of yours is just another loser."

"No, it isn't," Tommy said. "If they're only going to be interested in a guy who looks, acts, and thinks like their wonderful Cliff, then that's what they're gonna get!

Once they see he's not so special, they'll come running back."

"Then why didn't it work in the cafeteria just now?" Jason asked.

"Give it time," Tommy said. "Let's review and make sure we're doing everything right."

The boys stopped and drew their index cards from their pockets.

"Wear fisherman knit sweater," Jason read.

"Check," Tommy said.

"Use 'significant' and 'on the other hand' a lot," Mitch read.

"Check," Tommy said.

"Don't comb hair," Andy read.

"With those spikes and all the goop you use to make them stay that way, it looks like you spent two hours on your hair," Tommy complained to Andy.

"Well, I did, but at least I didn't *comb* it," Andy said. He pulled a few strands from the spike in the front and pressed them on his forehead. They ended up sticking straight out. "There, are you happy, Ryder?"

Tommy nodded and turned to Mitch. "Your hair looks too neat, too, Pauley."

Mitch reached up and rubbed his head vigorously. "It's hard to make hair this short look messy. But Coach says I gotta keep it short."

Tommy looked over Jason, whose red hair resembled a mop, as usual. "You're okay," Tommy said, absently roughing up his own sandy brown hair. He studied his card. "Wait! Here's what we *didn't* do. We didn't flash them smiles that show all of our teeth." Tommy looked up. "Here comes Jennifer. Let's give it a try."

Jennifer hurried down the main corridor toward her locker. Because they had taken the time to eat their sack lunches and discuss props, Jen and Randy had only been halfway through their second rehearsal when the end-of-lunch bell had rung. Randy had insisted they finish it, and now Jennifer was running late. She had three minutes to get her French book and make it upstairs to Mr. Armand's class.

She saw the boys standing in a little group and gave them an absentminded smile. To her surprise, all of them suddenly bared clenched teeth at her and grinned horrible grins that reminded her of jack-o-lanterns.

In a split-second Jennifer realized what they were doing and why. She caught her breath in a sob and fled past them. They're making fun of me! she thought, mortified. It's that blueberry muffin Jeff packed in my lunch. I bet my teeth are all blue!

She clamped her lips over them and

headed for the girls' bathroom with her head down. Now she was really going to be late! Jen found herself getting angry at Randy. He could have *told* her about her teeth! But, no, he'd just sat there staring at her as they rehearsed, probably feeling totally grossed-out the entire time. Why couldn't boys tell girls things like that? *She* would have told him if he'd had mustard on his chin or something . . . wouldn't she?

Fighting tears, Jennifer pushed through the door of the bathroom, wishing she carried a toothbrush in her purse, like Nora always did.

After school that day, Nora and Jennifer stood at their lockers selecting the books they'd need for the weekend's homework.

"I'm sorry I got mad at you this morning," Nora mumbled, not looking at Jennifer. "Actually, I wasn't as mad about your bringing candy as I was that you'd brought anything in the first place."

"I'm sorry I got mad at you, too," Jennifer muttered. "Maybe you didn't even know I was."

Nora faced Jen. "Of course I knew."

"Oh, Nora," Jennifer wailed, "I hate it when we get mad at each other!"

Nora nodded vigorously. "Me, too!" She

studied Jen's face worriedly. "But we're okay now, aren't we?"

"Sure we are!" Jennifer's face broke into a wide grin. "But only if you'll come over for dinner tonight. Then we can watch *Dallas* and have a long talk and — " She broke off with a sigh. "Doesn't it seem like forever since we had a long talk?"

"Yes, and I'd love to," Nora said. "In fact, if it's okay with you, I'll just go home with you now. I can call my mom from your house."

Susan came up to the girls, belting her long maroon wool coat and looking peeved, as usual. "Guess what I saw Mrs. Scott — " She stopped as Mr. Armand, the French teacher, joined the three of them.

"I meant to tell you after class today, Nora, that your zucchini casserole was very tasty," he said. "Very tasty indeed."

Nora's eyebrows shot up. "He — you ate it already?"

"Oh, sure, at lunch," Mr. Armand said. "Cliff — uh, Mr. Rochester brought it in and popped it into the microwave for a few minutes. Everybody loved it." He walked away muttering, "Very tasty, very tasty, indeed."

Susan patted Nora's shoulder. "I can sympathize, kid. I was about to tell you that I saw Mrs. Scott leave the teachers' dining room eating a scone. I bet Heathcliff didn't save *one thing* to share with his wife at home. I wonder why?"

Jennifer thrust her head into her locker, sure that Nora would be unable to resist making an "Edna" remark.

Nora didn't disappoint her. "Jeff says Cliff says Edna won't eat anything but raw meat since they moved here," Nora said solemnly. She slammed her locker door to cover the choking noises coming from Jennifer's locker.

Susan's face paled and her nose and mouth formed a "yuck!" expression.

Nora changed the subject quickly, afraid that she, too, was about to crack up. "Bet Cliff didn't pass around any of Tracy's blue cookies!" she said.

Susan laughed. "Maybe he could shellac them and donate them to the Christmas bazaar. Miss Jamison could sell them as paperweights!"

"Or we could ask the boys if they need some extra shot puts for phys. ed.," Nora said, putting on her oversized corduroy and satin baseball jacket.

Jennifer took out her identical jacket and closed her locker. "Speaking of the boys, I *got* the fisherman knit sweaters. But what's with those horrible faces they've been making all day? I mean, wait'll you hear what I *thought* they were doing it for!" Laughing, she leaned against her locker and described The Blueberry Muffin Blunder.

"But when I looked in the mirror in the bathroom," Jen finished, "my teeth were as clean as they were when I left the dentist yesterday morning!"

Jennifer waved a hand suddenly. "Shh! Here they come . . . and *they're doing it!*" Nora and Susan took a fast glance behind them. The three girls then collapsed into laughter, straightening up only once to exchange fierce, jack-o-lantern grimaces. That just made it worse. Nora actually felt tears running down her cheeks.

Jason, Tommy, and Mitch, still in their fisherman knit sweaters and with freshly messed-up hair, stopped a few yards away from the girls. As was the case every Friday afternoon, the main corridor had emptied out much sooner than it did on the other weekdays.

"They're laughing again!" Mitch hissed through his "Cliff smile."

"Not at us," Tommy said through his own Cliff smile. "Hit it, Jason."

Jason struck a teacherish pose with his head cocked thoughtfully and his arms folded across his chest, though his skateboard was tucked under one of them. "I think it's significant in Chapter Ten that Catherine and Edgar seem to be so happily married," he said loudly. "On the other hand, it's significant that when Heathcliff comes back, Catherine acts like she's pretty bored living at Thrushcross Grange."

He turned to see that the girls had stopped laughing. They were staring at him, wide-eyed. Then, in the same split second, the girls burst out laughing again.

"Would you mind telling us what is so funny?" Mitch shouted angrily.

Nora pointed at Jason, too helpless with laughter to speak.

"It's pronounced *grange*, stupid," Susan finally gasped, wiping her eyes. "Not gran-gee! It rhymes with *strange*, a word I'm sure you're familiar with!"

The girls continued to laugh as Mitch and Jason stomped off down the hall. Tommy looked after them, undecided as to what to do. Finally, he hurried after the other boys.

"Give it time!" Tommy pleaded with them.

Jason jetted off on his skateboard without a word.

Mitch peeled off his fisherman knit sweater and threw it at Tommy. "They were just laughing at another food joke, right, Ryder?" he shouted, tucking his white T-shirt into his jeans and shrugging into his letter sweater. "Well, I've got one for you: If you think we're gonna listen to any more of your advice, you're *nuts*."

Chapter 12

Jen, Nora, Jeff, and Jeff's girl friend Debby were sprawled across chairs, the couch, and the floor in the Manns' den that night, watching *Dallas*.

Listlessly, Nora picked up a few kernels of popcorn from the bowl in front of her on the coffee table and put them into her mouth, being careful not to crunch down too loudly. She didn't want to get a dirty look from one of the three avid *Dallas* fans who surrounded her.

Nora sighed. She let her mind drift back over the events of the day, especially what she and Jen were calling the "food fiasco." They'd managed to laugh about it on the way home from school, mostly because the boys' terrible Cliff imitations had made *everything* seem funny. Even through their laughter, however, Nora had felt the wall that had sprung up between the two of them since Cliff had entered their lives. A wall that said "We can laugh about this, but we can't really have a heart-to-heart talk about today's disaster or about anything else regarding Cliff." Nora was afraid to say too much about Cliff for fear that Jennifer would somehow use that information to get Cliff to like *her* better. Did Jennifer feel the same way? Probably. Why else did both of them keep finding excuses not to have the long talk Jen had mentioned that afternoon?

Nora stared hard at her best friend, who was idly braiding and unbraiding a section of her long black hair, eyes glued to the TV. The worst thing, Nora thought, was that she couldn't brainstorm with Jen — like they did on so many other things — about getting Cliff's attention. Because Jen wanted it, too!

Nora heaved sigh number seven. How much longer could this go on? Until Cliff finally made his preference known, she guessed. He still seemed undecided, focusing his dazzling smile on one of them one day and another the next. Cliff "Fickle" Rochester! Maybe what he needs is another little push, Nora decided.

She stood up suddenly. "Mind if I use the phone?"

The other three didn't even look at her. "Shh!" they said furiously.

"Thanks," Nora said cheerfully. She

went into the kitchen, closed the door behind her, and dialed a number.

"Sorry to call so late, Mrs. Crowley," she was soon saying to Steve's mother. "But I need to talk to Steve. It's urgent."

Steve took a long time coming to the phone. "Hi, Nora. What's up?" he said meekly. He'd heard about the "food fiasco" from Lucy Armanson.

"Oh, Steve, somehow, *four other girls* decided to bring Cliff food today," Nora told him. "You've got to help me!"

Steve let out his breath in a mixture of relief and guilt. So they weren't blaming him! "Four other girls?" Steve said, trying to inject a note of astonishment into his voice. "Gee, Nora, that's too bad."

"Not only that, but Cliff didn't even eat the stuff himself," Nora said. "I guess the teachers sort of made a party out of it."

"No wonder. Not having to eat cafeteria food is a reason to celebrate."

Nora didn't laugh. "Steve, you've *got* to come up with another way to get Cliff to like me the best and — "

"Oh, no!" Steve cut her off with a groan. "Nora — I'm dry. It was hard enough to come up with the food thing!"

Nora decided to try flattery. "Which was a *brilliant* idea, by the way. Even Sally said so. It wasn't your fault other people had the same idea."

"You told your sister? Then why don't you ask her to — "

"Because she's not a man," Nora snapped.

On the other end of the line, Steve was silently making a face at the receiver. *Nora* was the brilliant one, he was thinking. There she was, calling him a man again — she *knew* he couldn't turn her down now!

Back in the Manns' kitchen, Nora could hear the theme music of *Dallas* through the closed door. "All I'm asking is that you *try*," Nora begged hurriedly. "Pleeeeeease, Steve? I'm on my knees!"

Steve sighed. "Let me sleep on it, okay? I'll drop by your house tomorrow. IF I come up with anything, that is."

Nora was hanging up the phone when Jennifer came into the kitchen, carrying the bowl of popcorn. "You were on the phone?" Jen asked, her eyes wide with surprise.

"I asked, remember?" Nora said. She tried to change the subject. "Did you watch the previews? What's going to happen next week?"

Jen ignored the questions. "Who were you talking to?"

"Um, my mom," Nora said quickly. "I asked her to come and get me as soon as *Dallas* was over."

Jennifer's eyes narrowed suspiciously. "But you did that this afternoon!"

"It was just a reminder," Nora mumbled, eyes downcast. She felt rotten. This time, she hadn't merely withheld something from Jen, she'd told her an outright lie!

And Jennifer didn't believe it. But she decided not to press Nora any further. Things were tense enough as it was. "Then your mom will be here any second," she said. "So much for the long talk we were going to have."

"Well, you were the one who had to watch *Dallas*," Nora said.

"But you were the one who insisted we play Monopoly after dinner with Jeff and Debby," Jennifer shot back.

The two stared at each other sadly.

Jen sighed. All the secrets we're keeping from each other, she thought. All the sneaking around we're doing, all the things we aren't saying. . . . She put a few kernels of popcorn into her mouth. "I hate this," she said flatly.

"But it's Orville Redenbacher's," an offended Jeff said, coming into the kitchen.

"Me, too," Nora said. And she knew Jen wasn't talking about the popcorn, but about the wall.

Several blocks away, Steve Crowley was

pacing his bedroom floor, trying very hard not to panic, and feeling sorry for himself at the same time. Why me? he kept thinking. Why me — a guy who hasn't even had his first date yet? A guy with absolutely no experience?

What was he going to do? He was desperate! Was there any way he could call Ann Landers? Maybe she had an "800" number for emergencies. If she did, it would be in her column in tonight's paper. He flung open his bedroom door, rushed through the hall, and then leaped down the stairs.

Mrs. Jessop from across the street was watching *Falcon Crest* with Steve's mom in the family room. The two women often watched TV together because their husbands worked at night — Mr. Crowley at the family restaurant and Mr. Jessop as a disc jockey for Cedar Groves' classical music station.

Steve greeted Mrs. Jessop and then fell into a chair with the family section of the newspaper. There! He ran a finger through several letters and Ann's answers to them. At the bottom, all it said was *Write to Ann Landers in care of this newspaper.*

He was a dead man.

"I can't believe it!" Mrs. Jessop said, pointing at the TV screen. "I just read in *TV Guide* that that actress is only seventeen! And here they have her made up so that she looks thirty!"

"The producers probably felt they had to make her look older, Joyce," Steve's mom said. "I mean, in real life, such a distinguished professor wouldn't be interested in a teenager." She threw a slight smile at Steve, hoping he wasn't offended by the "teenager" remark.

He was staring at his mother, open-mouthed.

"Steve? What's the matter?"

Steve jumped out of his chair, ran over to her, and planted a resounding smack of a kiss on her cheek. "Mom, I love you! You just saved my life! And I will be eternally grateful to you for the rest of it!"

Mrs. Crowley laughed and shook her head. "Joyce, last night I gave him a twenty-dollar advance on his allowance and I didn't even get a thanks. Tonight, I barely smile at him and he's eternally grateful. Figure that out."

Mrs. Jessop laughed and shook her head, too. "Men!"

Steve flashed them a manly, dazzlingly self-confident smile and sauntered out of the room, the words *look older, look older, look older* echoing in his head.

"Look older, huh?" Nora said thoughtfully the next afternoon. She studied her face in the mirror on the wall of the Ryans' dining room. Smoothing her curly brown hair off her forehead and holding it at the top of her head, she turned to Steve. "What does this look like?"

He chugged down some of the milk she'd put in front of him. "A crewcut."

"I mean, does it make me look like an older woman?"

"Nope. It makes you look like a little boy," Steve said, reaching for another granola bar.

Nora sighed. "Oh, well, I'll figure out some way to look older. Thanks for the tip, Steve." She folded her arms on the table and rested her head on them.

"Tired already?" Steve asked. "It's only three o'clock."

"I'm tired of keeping secrets from Jennifer," Nora said. "That's what I'm tired of."

Steve stood up. "What can I say, kiddo? Except that all's fair in love and war."

Nora followed him out the front door. "What is it with you and these corny old lines?" she asked. " 'The way to a man's heart is through his stomach.' 'All's fair in love and war.' I'm going to start calling you Mr. Originality!"

Steve got on his ten-speed and grinned at her. "Sticks and stones may break my bones, but names will never hurt me!"

Nora groaned as he waved and pedaled away.

Meanwhile, at the Cedar Groves Animal Shelter, Jennifer was dialing Cliff's home phone number and taking deep, even breaths to calm herself down. One ring . . . two . . . three . . . four.

"Hello?" He sounded out of breath.

"Mr. Rochester?" Jen said. "This is Jennifer Mann and I'm a volunteer at the animal shelter, and I'm calling because I know you're an animal lover and I want to find out if you would consider adopting a cat because there are currently too many here and if some of them aren't adopted soon they'll have to be put to sleep and — "

"Oh, Jennifer, I'm sorry." Cliff interrupted. "But I had enough trouble getting my landlord to accept Edna. He'd never go for *two* cats."

"I understand," Jennifer mumbled.

Jennifer hung up a minute or so later feeling miserable. She was soon back on her knees, scrubbing out the cage she'd been working on before she got up the nerve to call Cliff. If he really liked me, if I was his favorite, he would have found some way to take an extra cat or two, she thought sadly. And it's not just the cats, either. Everything would be better if I could get him to like me the best. And it's the same old question: How can I do that?

How? she asked herself as she put the cleaning tools away.

How? she asked herself as she said good-bye to Becky, the shelter manager.

How? she asked herself as she stepped out of the building into the weak, late-afternoon sunshine.

And then she saw Steve riding by on his ten-speed.

"Steve!" she shouted joyfully, running to catch up.

Steve pulled over to the curb and groaned inwardly as he watched Jen race toward him from the animal shelter. When was he going to learn not to ride down this street on Saturday afternoons? No doubt Jen had animal shelter fever and was going to beg him to take yet another cat. And his mother would kill him if he did.

But when he heard what Jen wanted, he fervently wished that it *was* animal shelter fever.

"So, see, if you could just give me one more idea, *just* one," Jennifer was saying.

You'll never get away with giving them the same advice this time, Steve warned himself. You were just lucky that they didn't blame you for the food fiasco. Don't do it!

But then . . . what else could he do?

Sighing, Steve laid his bike against the curb and sat down next to it. "Well, Jen,

Cliff is ten years older than you are," Steve said. It was exactly the same way he'd begun his presentation to Nora only an hour earlier.

As Steve rode his bike home a few minutes later, he debated about what he figured were his only two choices. Should he ask his parents to let him transfer to the local private school? OR should he ask them to let him go live with his Uncle Roger in Los Angeles for a couple of years?

When he wheeled his bike into the Crowley garage, he found his dad assembling a birdhouse at his workbench.

"A pretty little blonde named Tracy came by here looking for you just a little while ago," Mr. Crowley said.

Steve gulped. Oh, no. Was Tracy going to ask —

"I told her you'd give her a call when you got home," Steve's dad went on cheerfully. "But you'd better call this Mia Stevens first." He took a slip of paper from his pocket and handed it to Steve. "She's called three times already."

"No!" Steve shouted. "Oh, please! No, no, no, no, no!" He pounded his fist on the workbench.

Mr. Crowley chuckled. "Like father, like son. I was a teenage heartthrob myself. Better get used to this, son."

Chapter 13

On Sunday night, Jennifer hung up her pink princess phone, propped a pillow behind her back, and picked up her diary.

I just got off the phone with Nora, she wrote. *We talked about Jeff and Debby and my little brother Eric and her big sister Sally and her mom's current court case and my dad's business trip and our French homework. In other words, we talked about everything but each other. And Cliff. That's the way it's been with us for weeks.*

At first, competing with each other — even being sneaky about it — was sort of fun. But now it's really starting to bother me. Like yesterday, I asked Steve for more advice and I've felt guilty about not telling Nora ever since. I had another chance to tell her when she called just now, but I didn't. I feel so disloyal. What kind of a friend am I, let alone a best friend?

Jennifer looked up at the ceiling and held her head back so that the sudden tears in her eyes wouldn't fall. After a minute, she bent back over her diary.

As punishment, I'm not going to use the advice Steve gave me, even though I think it's good advice. In fact, I'm going to call Nora right now and give the advice to her!

She picked up the phone again and dialed. Sally answered. "Oh, hi, Jen. Can you hold on a minute? You're not going to believe this, but Nora just went downstairs wearing one of my mom's dress-for-success suits, of all things."

Jennifer gasped. Nora was obviously planning to look older, too! How had she gotten wind of the idea? From Steve? Or had she come up with it on her own? That didn't matter. The important thing was that unlike her best friend Jennifer, Nora hadn't seen fit to share the idea!

Jen tried to keep the anger out of her voice. "Never mind, Sally. In fact, don't even bother telling Nora I called. I just wanted her help on a French verb, but I suddenly figured it out for myself."

She made herself hang the phone up gently. But she picked up her diary and printed: TWO CAN PLAY THIS GAME! Then she marched over to her closet and took her dressiest dress from the rod and held it up for inspection. It was a straight blue satin shift completely covered by a layer of lace. Jennifer thought it made her look about eight years old like most of the things her dad impulsively bought without consulting her first. She squinted at it critically, then held it against her body and looked in the mirror. Actually, she decided, it was the lace that made the dress look so little-girlish. With sudden excitement, Jennifer laid the dress on her bed and slid her hand between the lace and the satin. She was delighted to find that they were basted together only at the shoulders. Just a few snips . . . then, perhaps, a wide black belt . . . and maybe those high-heeled black pumps reserved for special occasions. . . .

Still in her pajamas the next morning, Jen put her cereal bowl in the sink and then quickly got her longest coat from the hall closet and rushed upstairs with it.

A half hour later, she came back down the stairs, coat buttoned to her neck, hood over her hair. She could hear Jeff washing the breakfast dishes in the kitchen.

" 'Bye, Jeff!" she called hurriedly, making straight for the front door. She had her hand on the knob when she heard his voice behind her.

"Do you have lunch money?" he asked.

She didn't turn around. "Got some, thanks," she muttered, opening the front door.

"Jennifer?" She felt his hand on her shoulder, then he was turning her around. "Jennifer? Are you —"

She looked up at him with a slight you-caught-me smile.

"What on earth —" he began. His startled eyes took in her face, then he pushed the hood off her head to reveal that her glossy black hair was pulled back tightly into a chignon.

"I decided to try wearing a new hairstyle and more makeup," Jen said sheepishly.

"*More* is one thing — a whole tube of blue eye shadow is quite another!" he said.

"It's not from a tube," Jen babbled. "It's powder — and the color's called 'Teasing Teal.' "

Jeff was squinting at her. "Eyeliner, too?"

"Uh-uh, eye *pencil*," Jen corrected. "It looks more natural than eyeliner, because you smudge it a little."

"But honey, are you supposed to smudge it out to your temples?" Jeff's look traveled down to her shiny black pumps. His expression changed abruptly. "All right, young lady!" he said sternly. "Unbutton that coat! On the double!"

With a number of very put-upon sighs, Jennifer did so. "There! Are you happy?" she snapped.

Jeff's eyes were wide with shock at the tightly cinched, laceless blue satin. "Jennifer Mann, you march right back up those stairs and change into something that's appropriate for junior high! You look like you're going to a . . . a . . . cocktail party!" he sputtered.

Jennifer knew her only chance lay in throwing herself on his mercy. "Oh, Jeff, please! Please! It's only for this one day. Just this once! *Please*?" Jennifer wailed. "Look — if you let me wear this just this once, I'll . . . I'll wear that hideous yellow slicker the next five times it rains, okay?"

Jeff stopped shaking his head and narrowed his eyes. "The next *ten* times!"

"Seven," Jennifer said.

"Deal," Jeff said. "But if you get sent home, I'm going to say you snuck out of here this morning, unseen."

Jennifer laughed. "Oh, Jeff, this is really *conservative* compared to what some people wear. The other day, Mia Stevens wore a blouse that I'm sure was just a plastic garbage bag with holes for her arms and head."

Jeff permitted himself a small smile. "Must have looked pretty trashy."

* * *

A half hour later, Jen had deposited her coat in her locker and was mincing toward the corridor that led to the teachers' parking lot. As she rounded the corner, she wasn't a bit surprised to see Nora, at the other end of the hall, wearing her mother's severely tailored gray flannel blazer and skirt with a white-bowed blouse and gray pumps. But Jen's mouth dropped open when she saw Susan, Mia, and Tracy.

Susan was wearing a dull-green shirtwaist dress and pearls, an outfit that instantly reminded Jennifer of June Cleaver, Beaver's mother. Susan's mousy-brown hair was gathered like Jen's into a knot at the back of her neck. She had painted perfect circles of bright-pink blush on her cheeks and was wearing at least three coats of black mascara.

Mia, on the other hand, was actually wearing less makeup than usual. Like Nora, Mia sported a dress-for-success-type suit, but hers was lime green. She had, for once, actually coordinated her hair color with something she was wearing. Spikeless and styled in a smooth French roll, it was the same watermelon-pink as her bowed blouse. Bright yellow pumps completed her look.

Tracy looked exactly the same as she always did, except she was wearing a huge pair of horn-rimmed glasses without lenses.

Unlike Friday morning's food fiasco, nobody was shouting or making accusations. "It *can't* be another coincidence. No way," Jen muttered, as she joined the silent, unhappy little group.

"That's already been established," Susan snapped.

Well, there's nothing we can do about it right now, Jen thought, and focused her attention on the door to the parking lot. She was still so mad at Nora that she allowed herself only one quick sideways glance at her from this new closeup angle. She saw that Nora was carrying one of her mother's old briefcases, and that she had smudged charcoal-gray eye shadow way out past the corners of her eyes. She looks like she has wings, Jen decided. And she looks ridiculous! Then she caught herself; did her own eye makeup look that weird? She'd smudged it out pretty far — even Jeff had said so.

Nora caught Jennifer's eyes on her. "I'm surprised Jeff let you out of the house like that!" she snapped.

"I'm surprised your mother let you wear her best suit!" Jennifer shot back.

Nora shrugged, as if it had been nothing. Actually, she'd had to beg her mother the night before, and it was only after Nora had promised to wash the kitchen floor every Saturday for six months that Mrs. Ryan had finally relented. "But no alterations!" she had ordered. That's why the waistband of the skirt was almost touching the bottom of Nora's bra. That's why Nora couldn't tuck the bowed blouse in. And that's why she had to keep the blazer on and buttoned up. She hoped it wouldn't be too warm in the classrooms today.

Suddenly, the door opened and Cliff entered the building with Mrs. Hogan, the drama teacher. He was immediately surrounded by the five girls. "Hi, Mr. Rochester!"

Cliff studied them, then looked over their heads at Mrs. Hogan, completely bewildered. "I thought you said the annual Drama Club production was in April, Claire!"

Mrs. Hogan nodded, the same look of confusion on her face. "Girls, you'll have to excuse us," she finally said, "but Mr. Rochester and I must attend a brief teachers' meeting before the first bell."

Speechless, dejected, the girls watched them hurry off down the hall. After a full minute of bleak silence, Jennifer spoke up. "He . . . he thought we were wearing costumes for a play," she said hoarsely. "He

. . . he thought — " Her voice broke. Don't cry, Jennifer, she ordered herself.

Susan was ripping out the bobby pins that held her hair in a bun. "It would have worked if the rest of you hadn't shown up looking like you're playing dress-up with Mommy's clothes!" she said angrily.

"You should talk!" Mia said. "Only it looks like your mommy is June Cleaver!"

Tracy giggled.

Susan whirled around and faced her. "And you! What's with the stupid glasses, anyway? I'm surprised Cliff managed to keep a straight face!"

Tracy frowned. "Steve said I needed to add a few years to my age, and — "

"He said look older," Susan snapped. "Not look ugly."

Susan and Tracy clapped their hands over their mouths at the same time. "Did I hear you right?" Susan asked from behind her hand. "*Steve* told you?"

Tracy nodded.

"But Steve told *me*!" Susan sputtered.

Nora waved her hands frantically. "Steve told *you*? Steve told *me*!"

Then someone brought up the subject of the food fiasco. And the one-syllable word "Steve" was hissed again and again and again with increasing indignation.

Like most of the rest of the eighth-graders, Steve was at that very minute hanging out on the school's front steps, waiting for the first bell to ring. His friend Jim Blake waved to him from the sidewalk and leaped up the steps to join him.

"You feeling okay?" Jim asked. "You look kind of sick."

Steve gave him a wry smile. "I *feel* kind of sick. But don't worry. It's not catching. This is the way any guy looks three hours before he's scheduled to be executed."

"What are you talking — " Jim started to ask. He was interrupted by the sound of pounding footsteps and then five girls bursting through the school's heavy front doors. "There he is!" they shouted.

Oh, terrific, Steve thought as they advanced on him. And I thought I had at least until lunch to live.

"It was nice knowing you," Steve said to Jim, who took one look at the angry mob and fled.

"How could you do this to me!" Nora shouted. "Some friend you are!"

"Just how long did you think you'd get away with this little game?" Susan demanded. "Giving all of us the same advice not once but *twice*!"

"I trusted you!" Jennifer wailed. "I trusted you, and look what happened!"

Suddenly, Steve felt himself growing

144

angry — and not just because practically everyone in the whole eighth grade was watching the humiliating scene. What made him madder was that these girls were being so *unfair* about his attempts to be *fair*! On top of that, he was surprised to find himself feeling a little *jealous* as he took in their elaborate clothes, hairstyles, and makeup. No girl had ever gone to that much trouble for *him*!

"You're a rat!" Susan concluded, turning on her heel and storming away.

"A traitor!" Nora added, joining her.

"A weakling!" according to Tracy.

"A preppie!" Mia contributed.

Jennifer had never been good at name-calling. She simply stuck her tongue out at him and flounced away.

Steve just stood there looking after them, red-faced, fists clenched.

Mitch Pauley and Tommy Ryder strolled past him. "Tough luck, Crowley," Mitch said.

"Yeah, looks like you're the scapegoat for *Cliffie's* lack of interest," Tommy added. "I wouldn't let 'em get away with it, if I were you."

Steve stared at them thoughtfully. "I don't intend to," he said slowly. "But I think I need some help. Give me a few hours to think about it. What do you say we get together for a little meeting at lunch?"

Chapter 14

After school that day, Nora stood in front of her open locker, eyes tearing. If you're going to cry, she ordered herself, at least wait until you're outside the building.

But she couldn't leave yet. Though she'd been standing there for ten minutes, she wanted to give Jennifer just one more minute. If Jen didn't show up by the end of that minute, Nora would know for certain — they were having a *real* fight.

Sure, she'd been mad at Jen this morning for the same reason she was sure Jen was mad at her — for being sneaky about the look-older idea. Actually, for being sneaky about *everything* lately. But, oh, how she wanted to tell Jennifer that she'd regretted her anger all day. And that she had spent the whole weekend feeling guilty. And that that morning's disaster had been the last straw. Nora was *through* with hiding things from her best friend.

Now maybe it was too late. After the confrontation with Steve, Jennifer hadn't said another word to Nora all day. Not even in the cafeteria.

Nora stuck her head in her locker as the tears began to fall. For years, she had prided herself on *never* having cried at school — not even in kindergarten. But here she was crying for the second time in a week . . . and with no tissue and rivers of gray eye makeup threatening her mother's best suit.

"Nora?"

Nora whirled around. Jennifer stood behind her, holding out a wad of tissue. Silent but relieved, Nora took it from her and mopped her face.

"I . . . I was looking for Randy Phillips," Jennifer explained. "I, um, changed some of my lines in the script and decided I'd better show it to him."

Nora just nodded, sniffling.

Suddenly, Jennifer's face crumpled, and she, too, looked on the verge of tears. "Oh, Nora, that wasn't it!" she burst out. "I . . . I . . . I'm never again going to hide anything from you!"

Nora grabbed her hands. "Me, neither! That's what I wanted to say, too! No more secrets!"

"Except for birthday and Christmas

presents," Jennifer added, beginning to smile.

All of a sudden, Jason Anthony careened around the corner on a collision course with Jen and Nora. He bailed off his skateboard, and Jennifer and Nora leaped apart. The skateboard crashed against a locker, flipped over, and stopped harmlessly on its back, wheels spinning.

Jason picked it up. "Pardon me, ladies. That was grievously inexcusable." With a polite smile, he backed away.

"*Grievously*?" the girls said to each other in unison, then cracked up.

Nora wiped her eyes. "Anyway, Jen, I'd love it if from now on we approach this Cliff project as a team. You know, like we do everything else. What do you think?"

Jennifer nodded. "I've been thinking about it all day, and I decided that I really wouldn't like it if he liked me better than you. In fact, I'd probably feel terrible. What I *would* like is if he liked me *and* you better than the other girls."

"We'll find a way," Nora said, grinning.

Jennifer worked the combination on her locker and opened it. "Let's go over to my house and cook up some plans."

"Only if you'll lend me something to wear," Nora said, pulling at the waistband on the gray flannel skirt. "This thing is so hot and itchy."

"You can wear those old Calvin Kleins that are too short for me," Jen said. "And I for one can't wait to get out of these pinchy shoes and into my Reeboks. You know, I really should try to find Randy first. I really did change the script a little."

"Oh, Jen, he's probably gone by now," Nora said, closing her locker. She closed Jennifer's, too, then linked arms with her. "Come on, let's go. Stay tuned, folks, for another Ryan and Mann Brainstorming Session."

"Got that right," Jen said, as the two started down the hall. "Two heads are better than one—that's our motto."

"Except when one of the heads is *Steve's*," Nora said, with a hint of the indignation she'd felt that morning. She pushed open the school's heavy front door.

"Speak of the devil," Jennifer whispered.

Steve was standing near the front steps with Tommy Ryder and Mitch Pauley, who was bouncing a basketball.

"Have you guys seen Randy Phillips?" Jen called to them.

Mitch stopped bouncing the ball. "I regret to say that I haven't seen the gentleman, Miss Mann."

"Nor have I, unfortunately," Tommy added.

Steve stood very straight. "I believe his

last class is drafting, Miss Mann. Perhaps you could check there."

Then the three boys bowed slightly and went into the building.

Jennifer and Nora stopped and burst out laughing as soon as the door closed behind the boys. *"Now what?"* they finally managed to gasp to each other at the same time.

"Was Mitch trying for an English accent, or does he just have a cold?" Nora sputtered, and Jennifer howled.

They were unaware that the boys had left the front door cracked open slightly and were listening just inside. Jason had joined them, skateboard tucked under his arm.

"They're laughing!" Mitch said to Steve.

"They laughed at me, too," Jason said, scowling.

"I told you to expect that at first," Steve said calmly.

Tommy took out a comb and pulled it through his sandy brown hair. "This plan doesn't make any sense, Crowley," he said. "I think it would be better if we — "

"Do us a favor and stop thinking, Ryder," Steve said. "That's what produced two loser plans before, remember?"

"What makes you so sure your plan isn't a loser, too?" Tommy demanded.

"I told you — experience," Steve explained patiently. "My parents used to do this to my brother and me whenever we made them mad. You know, like when we were fighting too much or wouldn't clean up our rooms. They would go around the house saying the bare minimum to us, and being really, really polite. At first, we'd think it was funny and kind of nice. I mean, anything's better than being yelled at, right?"

"Right," the other guys said.

"*Wrong*," Steve said. "After a couple of days — sometimes even after just a couple of hours — my brother and I would be going *crazy*. We'd be begging them to yell at us, spank us, *anything* but that."

"But *why* does it work?" Tommy asked.

Steve shrugged. "I don't know. All I know is that it does. Just trust me, okay? And keep it up. Are you with me?"

There was a moment of silence as the boys all looked at each other and thought it over.

"Okay," Tommy finally said. "Absolutely."

"Totally," Mitch agreed.

"Grievously," Jason said, nodding. "Whatever that means."

A few minutes later, Jennifer was unlocking the side door of the Manns' house.

"Jeff?" she called, as she and Nora walked into the kitchen. There was no answer. She shrugged and dropped her books on the kitchen table. "Must be out shopping or something." Both girls kicked their shoes off.

Jennifer went to the refrigerator and found a Coke for herself and a grapefruit juice for Nora. "Let's go upstairs."

Nora followed her out of the kitchen. They were on the stairs, shoes and drinks in hand, when they heard a key click in the side door and then the door being opened. "Anybody home?" Jeff hollered.

Jennifer had opened her mouth to answer him when she and Nora heard another voice.

"You keep this big place clean, Jeff? I have a hard enough time with a three-room apartment."

Cliff!

Nora and Jennifer turned to each other, wide-eyed. Neither could move another muscle.

"Jennifer?" Jeff called out again.

"Yes, you'd better make sure she's not here," Cliff said quickly. "She's part of what I wanted to talk to you about."

This time, the girls mouths dropped open as they stared at each other. *Cliff came to tell Jeff how much he likes me!* Jen thought, and Nora was thinking the same thing.

"Well, her books are here, so I'd better go make sure she's not," Jeff said. "Just let me put the kettle on and — "

"I really don't have time for tea," Cliff interrupted. "I'm supposed to meet a friend at Greatneck Park at four. We're going to start jogging together every day."

Without a word to each other, as if they were robots who had been programmed with exactly the same instructions, Nora and Jen immediately tiptoed down the stairs and slipped silently into the dining room and under the table, which was covered with an almost floor-length tablecloth.

A second later, Jeff came through the room and went up the stairs. They heard him knock on Jennifer's door and open it. Then he returned to the kitchen. "The coast is clear," he said to Cliff. "Now, what's the problem? You sounded pretty upset when you called at noon."

Cliff sighed. "Well, Jeff, it seems that I've become an object of adoration for a big chunk of the eighth-grade female population, including your Jennifer and Nora Ryan. And it's becoming a problem."

Nora and Jennifer gripped each other's hands so tightly that it hurt.

Jeff was chuckling. "They made a few adoring noises on your first day, but I had no idea it had developed into a full-fledged teacher crush. I suddenly understand a whole bunch of strange actions on Jennifer's part of late. But look, I wouldn't worry about it, Cliff. I'm sure every young male teacher goes through this. It's almost like an initiation."

"I didn't worry about it at first," Cliff said. "I mean, I thought it was just temporary and kind of cute. I was even a little flattered by it. But today Claire Hogan, the drama teacher, said something that really got me worried."

"What'd she say?" Jeff asked.

"Well, see, the girls have been bringing me little gifts and waiting to walk with me and so forth for a few weeks now," Cliff explained. "And the other teachers, of course, couldn't help but notice that. Then today . . . uh . . . I guess the girls decided to make themselves look older for my sake . . . and . . . and when Claire saw that. . . . Well, she said that if they were going to *that* much trouble . . . well, then, I must be *encouraging* them!"

Jeff snorted. "Oh, hogwash!"

"Right! I'm doing nothing! And I know that, and you know that, but the parents of these girls don't know that." Cliff sighed. "What if one of those parents gets the same idea that Claire has? That I'm *encouraging* his or her daughter? Jeff, I could lose my job!"

"Now, Cliff, listen here — "

"What am I going to do?" Cliff wailed.

"You're going to do *nothing*, just as you have been," Jeff said firmly. "You're just going to have to let it burn out on its own. And it will! You were trained to teach junior high, Cliff! Didn't they teach you anything about thirteen-year-old girls? Thirteen-year-old girls are just starting to think about dating and . . . well, hey, it wasn't that long ago for you yourself, my boy! It's *scary*, don't you remember?"

Cliff laughed a little.

"So what do girls do?" Jeff continued. "They start trying out their new feelings on some safe, older guy they know would *never* return those feelings. That would *really* be scary."

Jen and Nora exchanged outraged looks.

Cliff whistled. "Were you a psychology major in college, Jeff?"

"No. I just know kids. The point is, the girls will lose interest in you as they feel more *comfortable* with boys their own age," Jeff said gently.

The girls heard a chair scrape as Cliff stood up, ready to leave. "I . . . I hope you're right, Jeff," he said slowly. "And I hope they lose interest *soon*."

"Come on. I'll go out with you," Jeff said.

Chapter 15

Nora was the first to finally crawl out from under the table in a dining room that was almost dark in the deepening twilight. Smoothing the wrinkles out of her gray flannel skirt, she padded on stockinged feet to the kitchen. She picked up the phone, called her mother's office, and, in as few words as possible, asked to be picked up on her mother's way home from work. Hanging up the receiver, she didn't turn around, even when she heard Jennifer come into the kitchen.

A long minute of silence ticked by. Neither girl moved.

Finally, Nora whirled around. "Jeff should talk about hogwash!" she burst out. "What's hogwash is his theory about why we like Cliff!"

"Yeah!" Jennifer said. "*I'm* not uncomfortable with boys my age!"

"Me, neither!" Nora said. "Jeff makes me so mad!"

Jennifer nodded vigorously. "Me, too — and Cliff makes me even madder! Why did he have to pick *Jeff* to talk to? How humiliating! How am I ever going to face Jeff now?"

Nora shrugged. "I don't know, but you'll have to. And the toughest thing is that you'll have to pretend like you never heard a word. I mean, he'd kill us if he ever found out we were eavesdropping."

Jennifer struggled to find yet another reason to be mad at Cliff and Jeff. But she could no longer hold back the pain. "Oh, Nora, I thought he *liked* me!" It came out as a sob.

Nora's eyes also filled with misery. "I thought he liked me, too!" she wailed.

Suddenly, Nora said, "Wait a minute, Jen! You know what? We're jumping to the wrong conclusion! I bet he really *does* like us. Notice how he never told Jeff he *didn't*!"

Jennifer nodded a little.

"Well, then, don't you see?" Nora demanded. "He's just afraid to *show* us how much he likes us because he's afraid, like he said, that he'll lose his job! That's what this is *really* all about."

"I'm sure you're right," Jennifer said. "What a relief!"

"Yeah, I feel much better, too," Nora said.

But neither of them could manage to smile.

At that same minute, Susan was hurrying home through the thick stand of trees at the south end of Greatneck Park. The park was just about the only expanse of unpaved land left in Cedar Groves, and Susan figured it was about as close to the moors of England as she was going to get. For that reason, she liked to come here and daydream about Heathcliff.

Suddenly, Susan heard a woman's high-pitched laugh. She glanced over her shoulder and saw a couple of joggers about to enter the stand of trees. The woman wore a kelly-green velour warmup suit; the man wore a gray sweat shirt and matching sweat pants.

Heathcliff! Susan thought, darting behind a tree. And Edna! Finally, the infamous Edna! She must be getting better if Cliff's allowing her to be out in public jogging.

Susan peeked from behind the tree as the two came closer. Edna was gorgeous, with long auburn hair tied back in a ponytail and big eyes the color of her warmup suit.

To Susan's dismay, Edna stopped right in front of the tree where Susan was hiding.

"Look, Cliff!" Edna said. "Look at that birdie up on that branch!"

Heathcliff laughed. "You're just trying to find an excuse to stop. Come on, my girl, one more mile to go!" He grabbed her hand and forced her to keep jogging.

If the two had turned around, they would have seen Susan step from behind the tree and stare after them, her face pinched with disgust.

That night, Jennifer made herself get up in the middle of *Kate and Allie* and go up to her room. For the first time ever, she really didn't *want* to write in her diary, but she knew she had to. She knew there were things she *had* to say to herself, even though she didn't want to hear them.

Sitting cross-legged on her bed, she made herself record as much of the conversation between Jeff and Cliff as she could remember. Then she drew a line underneath it and started a fresh page.

During dinner tonight, she wrote, *Jeff didn't mention that Cliff had been here, and he acted like everything was normal. I caught him staring at me once, but I think that was because I was so much quieter than usual.*

You might think I was so quiet because I was still embarrassed and mad and sad like I was when Nora was here. But the truth is, I've been feeling more guilty than anything else. I never dreamed Cliff would suffer because of my behavior. To think that he's worried about losing his job . . . and I'm partly to blame!

Jen dropped her pen and covered her eyes. After a minute, she rubbed her temples, picked up the pen, and forced herself to go on.

The other thing I want to say is that I still disagree with Jeff's theory that we like Cliff because we're nervous about boys our own age. But — and this is the hardest thing of all for me to admit — I do think he was right about one thing. I wouldn't like it if Cliff ever did start liking me in a romantic way. I've been thinking about it for the last hour . . . and actually, the idea is scary! I'm sure Cliff has a lot of experience with dating, but I don't! What would I find to say to him if we were on a date? We couldn't talk about whales all that time! Or cats! Or teachers, because he is one! And what if he expected me to kiss him? I mean, I haven't even held hands with a boy yet!

Suddenly, Jennifer scooted across the bed and picked up the phone. Nora answered on the first ring.

"What are you doing?" Jen asked.

"Just sitting in my room, thinking." Nora sounded depressed.

"Me, too," Jennifer said. There was a long silence. "Nora?"

"Yeah?"

"We were lying to ourselves this afternoon," Jen said gently. "He doesn't like us. Not the romantic way, I mean."

"I know," Nora said in a tiny voice.

"And Nora . . . honestly . . . aren't you . . . aren't you glad that he doesn't? Wouldn't you be kind of scared if he did?"

There was another long, long silence. And then Nora sighed. "Yes," she said. "You know something, Jen? We haven't even dated a guy with a *part-time* job yet, let alone a guy who's worried about losing a *full-time* job!"

"We haven't dated anyone, *period*!" Jen said.

And then they were both laughing.

"Oh, Nora," Jennifer finally gasped, "I'm glad it's over!"

"From now on," Nora said, "Cliff is just our English teacher, okay?"

"*Cliff*? Oh, you mean *Mr. Rochester*!" Then Jennifer turned serious. "Do you think he'll get fired?" she asked worriedly.

"Not now, since almost half of his fan club quit," Nora said. "Maybe more than half. Didn't you hear what Mia said at lunch today? She said she must have been temporarily insane when she put her hair in a French roll. And that *no* guy was worth that! In fact, she left the cafeteria early. Said she was going to the cooking lab to ask Miss Morton if she could borrow some egg white."

"For what?"

"I guess when you're in a pinch, you can use it to put spikes in your hair."

Then Nora said, "What are you wearing tomorrow?"

"I don't know yet," Jen said, "but I *can* tell you that it'll be comfortable, it won't require heels, and it won't be blue!"

Nora started laughing again. "Oh, Jennifer, doesn't it feel good to get back to normal?"

The girls talked a little longer before saying good-bye. Then, on impulse, Nora picked up the phone again and dialed.

"Steve? It's Nora. I wanted to say I'm sorry that we ganged up on you this morning. I know you were only doing your best . . . and that we've been acting pretty weird lately. You'll be glad to know that we — at least Jen and I — are finished with — "

"Apology accepted," Steve interrupted in a pleasant tone. "And now, regrettably, I must go." *Click.*

Regrettably? Nora stared at the receiver. Regrettably, she thought, not everything is back to normal.

Chapter 16

The next morning, Tommy Ryder strutted down the walkway that connected the junior high with the high school. He felt terrific, being almost positive that a group of high school girls had just whistled at him. He'd been unable to confirm it, of course. Turning around when someone whistled at you was terribly uncool — it was like admitting you weren't used to it.

He had his second pleasant surprise of the day when he approached the junior high's front steps. There were Nora Ryan and Jennifer Mann, diehard members of the Cliff Hangers! For the first time in weeks, they weren't already inside the building, waiting for *Cliffie*. Had Cliffie finally ordered them to give him some space?

Tommy was just about to call out a remark to that effect when he remembered Steve's plan. Pasting a pleasant smile on his handsome face, he simply nodded at the girls as he strolled past.

"Tommy?" Nora called after him.

He stopped and turned around. "Yes, Miss Ryan?"

"Did Mr. Armand assign the next two sections in the French book or the next three?" she asked. "Jen says two; I say three."

"Two, I believe," Tommy said crisply. "But I shall check to be sure." He opened his notebook and scanned a page. "Yes, indeed, two is correct, Miss Ryan." With another nod, he smiled briefly and sailed away.

"What's with him?" Nora asked irritably. "What's with *all* of the guys, in fact?"

Jennifer giggled. "When we saw them after school yesterday, I thought they might be imitating Heathcliff in the book, especially because Mitch seemed to be trying for an English accent. But Heathcliff was usually *rude*, not polite."

"Yeah, it's more like they're imitating Miss Manners." Nora said. "How weird."

The bell rang, and Nora and Jennifer headed for the front door in the middle of the eighth-grade throng.

"It feels good to be out here before school again!" Nora shouted to Jen.

Jennifer nodded and laughed. "I was

beginning to miss freezing to death every morning!"

Mitch Pauley and Tommy Ryder were standing out in front of room 332 when Jen and Nora got there for homeroom. "Hi, Mitch," they said together.

"How did yesterday's basketball game go?" Nora asked him.

Jennifer smiled up at him shyly. "Did we win?"

"Thank you for your interest, Miss Ryan, Miss Mann," he said, nodding at each of them in turn. "We won eighty-six to seventy-eight."

Nora beamed. "Hey, that's terrif — " She broke off. The boys had already bowed slightly and gone inside the classroom. Nora and Jennifer looked at each other.

"I sort of expected to hear how many free throws were scored and how many timeouts there were," Nora said. "You know, the usual twenty-minute Mitch Pauley Basketball Recap."

Jennifer shook her head, equally puzzled. "Maybe they're having a special unit on etiquette in phys. ed.," she said. "Like the one we had on hygiene."

Inside the classroom, Mitch was playfully socking Tommy on the shoulder. "It's working!" Mitch crowed.

"What's with the English accent, if that's what yours is supposed to be?"

Tommy asked, a little irritably. It made him jealous when girls expressed an interest in Mitch's sports. "Americans can be polite, too, you know."

Meanwhile, Mia rushed into her own homeroom and found Andy already in his front-row seat. Mia stopped in front of him and twirled around. "What do you think?" she asked breathlessly. "I had to get up at *five* to make sure it'd be done on time!" Her hair was a mass of tiny spikes with just the tips sprayed either gold or silver.

Andy was impressed. But "It looks nice, Miss Stevens," was all he said.

"*Nice?*" Mia sputtered. "Is that all you can say? I don't want it to look *nice*! I didn't spend three hours for *nice*!"

Andy smiled politely. "It looks nice, Miss Stevens," he repeated. Then he pointed to the front of the room, where Mr. Robards, their homeroom teacher, had just arrived. "I think Mr. Robards will be wanting our attention now," he said softly.

Furious, Mia whirled around and flounced to her seat.

In English a few hours later, Mitch watched Rochester pace the front of the classroom. The teacher's face was flushed with emotion. "Now, also in Chapter Twenty-seven, Heathcliff tells Cathy that she will be forced to stay at Wuthering

Heights until her father dies, unless she marries Linton!" he said dramatically. "In other words, she may never again see her very ill father alive! Who can tell me why it is of utmost importance to Heathcliff that Cathy marry Linton? Why will his plans be ruined if she doesn't?"

To Mitch's surprise, not one of the Cliff Hangers was waving her hand frantically. In fact, not one had her hand up at all. With raised eyebrows, he glanced across the aisle and saw that Tommy was wearing the same astonished expression.

Mr. Rochester seemed a bit surprised himself. "No volunteers? Well, then, surely with her excellent grasp of this novel, Susan can fill us in."

Susan's head shot up, as if she'd been sleeping. "Huh? Oh, I'm sorry Mr. Rochester. I guess I wasn't paying attention."

Four boys gasped out loud.

Mitch, Tommy, Jason, and Andy joined Steve at a table in the cafeteria at noon that day to swap success stories. After hearing about Susan's lack of attention in English, Steve clapped his hands together and shook them over his head triumphantly. "All *right*! What'd I tell you guys? Those girls are spending so much time wondering and worrying about the way we're acting that Cliffie's been pushed aside. Now keep it up, okay? We may have won the battle, but we haven't won the war yet. Or however the saying goes."

Jason nodded and left the group to get in the food line. Sliding his tray along the stainless-steel dividing rail, he found himself directly behind Susan Hillard.

Susan was holding up the line, unable to make up her mind. Today the cafeteria was actually offering a choice of entrees: greasy-looking fried chicken and mashed potatoes or macaroni and cheese that lay steaming in what looked like a solid, inseparable glop.

"What'll it be?" asked the cafeteria worker, a spatula in each hand. "You're holding up the line, dearie."

Susan's face brightened when she spotted Jason behind her. He was something of an expert on cafeteria food, having sampled most of it . . . with his fingers, of course. "Have you ever tried the cafeteria's version of macaroni and cheese?" she asked him.

"I'm sorry, but I *cahn't* recommend it," he said, nose in the air. "Would you mind terribly if I went around you? I'm not having an entree." Only instead of "ontray," he pronounced it "entry."

Susan didn't laugh. In fact, she was still scowling as she made her way to the girls' usual center table with a plate of fried chicken and mashed potatoes. Jennifer, Nora, Tracy, and Mia were already seated.

"Would somebody tell me what's with those weirdos?" Susan asked irritably, slamming her tray down and nodding toward the boys' table, where Jason was just sitting down. "This veddy-veddy polite stuff is getting on my nerves!"

Mia nodded. "Veddy-veddy polite is veddy-veddy boring."

Tracy had to cut her solid mass of macaroni and cheese with a knife. Finally forking a bite-sized piece into her mouth, she looked up to see Mr. Rochester crossing the cafeteria. She swallowed and sighed loudly. "Have you ever seen anybody look so good in a fishnet sweater?"

Susan followed Tracy's gaze. "No, but speaking of veddy-veddy boring, Mr. Rochester *could* wear something else every once in a while, just for a change," she snapped. "I mean, since we have to look at him for an hour every day, he could at least try to provide some variety."

Jen and Nora exchanged looks of amazement. So Susan was over Mr. Rochester, too!

Tracy, however, gasped. "How can you say such a mean thing about Cliff? Don't you like him anymore?"

Susan picked up a chicken leg and took a tiny bite out of it. "Let's just say I'm glad he doesn't like *me*," Susan said slowly. "And I'll tell you why. Yesterday, I saw him jogging in Greatneck Park with his wife, Edna — "

Nora gave Jen a swift kick under the table. Jen bit her lip hard and refused to look at Nora.

". . . And I actually heard Edna call a bird a 'birdie'!" Susan continued in a disgusted voice. "She's not crazy, she's just *stupid*. And if that's the kind of birdbrain he goes for, I'm *flattered* that he never went for me!"

"Jeff says Edna does a lot of birdwatching," Nora said solemnly.

Jennifer shoved half of an apple in her mouth to keep from laughing. So Nora planned to maintain The Great Edna Myth forever!

"Jeff also says Edna caught a bird once in the patio of the Rochesters' apartment building and ate it before Cliff could stop her!" Nora continued, straight-faced.

The chicken leg Susan was holding slipped from her fingers. Her face was frozen in a "yuck!" expression.

Tracy's blue eyes were wide with confusion. "What's so stupid about seeing a birdie in the park? I've seen hundreds of birdies there!"

That comment gave Nora and Jen the excuse to double over and laugh until they felt light-headed. When Jennifer finally straightened up, she found Steve standing next to her.

"Miss Mann? I saw Randy Phillips in physical education earlier today and was asked to relay a message from him about your plans to meet briefly after school. Regrettably, he will be detained in shop for — "

"Stop it!" Nora suddenly shouted. "If I hear one more *regrettably*, I am going to scream. I am absolutely going to go loony tunes!"

Steve tried to look puzzled. "Regrettably, I don't understand — "

Susan slammed her hands over her ears. "No more! Please, no more! Don't you dare gush one more polite word, Steve!"

Jennifer looked at Nora and Susan and then up at Steve. "All right, *Mr.* Crowley, you win," she said calmly. "What is it you want? What will it take to make you guys act normal again?"

"Not necessarily *normal*," Mia said quickly, her eyes on Andy across the room, "but like your old selves?"

"If you'll give me a minute, ladies, I'll excuse myself to confer with my associates." Steve left quickly, to hide a victorious smile, but was back in less than a minute with Mitch, Tommy, Andy, and Jason.

The girls looked at them expectantly.

Tommy cleared his throat. "We shall reconsider our position, ladies, on one condition."

There was a long minute of silence.

"Well?" Susan snapped. "We're waiting."

Mitch bowed. "We never again want to hear the names 'Cliff' or 'Rochester' outside of that teacher's classroom."

"Deal," Nora, Jen, Susan, and Mia said immediately.

"Deal," Tracy said.

Then everybody was smiling at everybody else.

Andy dropped into the chair next to Mia's, and the two gazed happily into each other's eyes.

Jason jabbed his fingers in and out of Susan's mashed potatoes. Licking his fingers, he repeated the action.

"Grossness plus!" Susan shrieked.

Jen and Nora exchanged grins that read, Now EVERYTHING is back to normal . . . and I'm glad.

"Jason," Nora said cheerfully, "Why don't you go jump off a *cliff*?"

What happens when the students take over? Read Junior High #3, THE DAY THE EIGHTH GRADE RAN THE SCHOOL.